ERIK THERME

MORTOM

 THOMAS & MERCER

Text copyright © 2015 Erik Therme

Published by Thomas & Mercer, Seattle

www.apub.com

Amazon, the Amazon logo, and Thomas & Mercer are trademarks of Amazon.com, Inc., or its affiliates.

ISBN-13: 9781477829394
ISBN-10: 1477829393

Cover design by David Drummond

Library of Congress Control Number: 2014957290

Printed in the United States of America

To my wife, Shea,
for her endless support and patience

SUNDAY

1

At first glance, Andy Crowl thought they had the wrong house: The property at 21 Abel Avenue looked as if it had been vacant for weeks, not days. Two garbage cans lay overturned by the mailbox, a nest of rolled-up newspapers had collected by the front steps, and the lawn was easily overgrown by a foot. Something that resembled a station wagon was parked in the gravel beside the driveway. All four wheels were missing, and the front end had been stripped to the frame.

"This could be interesting," said Kate.

Andy cut the engine. "We're sure this is the place?"

"Directions were dead on. What time are we meeting the bank manager again?"

"Five o'clock on the *buttonhole*."

Kate raised her eyebrows. "Buttonhole?"

"Trust me, if Thatcher is half as pompous in person as he was on the phone, it's going to be a fun-filled hour. The little twit even instructed me to bring along three forms of identification."

He unzipped his bag and thumbed through the papers inside. The last two days were still a blur of e-mails and faxes, and it would be a miracle if he had remembered everything.

"Remind me to get copies of anything I sign—" he began, then realized Kate was gone. He opened his door and saw her standing on the front step.

"Door's open," she called down.

"Of course," he said under his breath. "The locals probably have a meth lab inside already."

He started up the driveway and cast a curious glance at the moped leaning against the garage. Ugly knots of rust had overtaken part of the metal frame, but it looked like it had been recently washed and waxed.

"Can I go inside?" Kate asked.

"I thought you said it was open."

"Yeah, but do you think it's okay to go in while we wait?"

"Go," he said irritably. "It's—"

The screen door slammed shut. He stared at the moped a moment longer, wondering if it had been abandoned on the property after Craig had died. Whatever the case, it was just more junk to deal with.

He was halfway up the steps when Kate burst back out. "I wouldn't go in there if I were you."

"Why?"

"Just don't say you weren't warned."

He opened the door and winced. "What's that lovely smell?"

"I don't know, but it's twice as bad upstairs."

"What is it? Spoiled food or something?"

She only shrugged. He took a cautious step inside the foyer and sniffed. Whatever it was, he had smelled worse. Not by much.

"Divide and conquer?" he proposed.

"Meaning?"

"I'll check the kitchen for stink bombs while you start opening windows." He offered a dry smile. "Or we can stand here and discuss how you're getting back home, since I'm the one here with the vehicle."

She sighed. "I so hate you right now."

"I know. And if we don't make it back out, remember that Mom always loved me best."

"You wish."

He took the staircase in a jog and squared off at the kitchen entrance. There was no question the smell was coming from inside—it was strong enough to knot his stomach.

Kate clapped his shoulder as she passed. "Have fun."

He ignored her and went to the fridge, almost afraid to look. To his surprise the power was on and the shelves were bare.

"Could it be a backed-up sewer?" Kate asked from the living room. "Didn't that happen to you and Carol a few years ago?"

"Twice." He tried the kitchen faucet and groaned when water ran out. "Utilities are on. Twenty bucks says they try and stick me with the bills."

"At least you can afford it now."

"Only if the place sells. The other option is to burn it all down and collect insurance money. I'll give you half if you help."

She appeared in the doorway. "Funny. What's the plan after Mr. Thatcher leaves? We eating, or visiting Mary?"

"Count me out of the latter."

"Andy, we have to pay our respects."

He checked the oven with a frown. "You go if you want. She likes you."

"She likes you, too," Kate said without conviction.

"Uh-huh. Regardless, I'm not going anywhere until I figure out—"

"Did you check under the fridge?"

He followed her finger. Most refrigerators had a plastic grate running across the bottom, but this one had been removed. The gap was at least three inches high—plenty of room for God knew what.

"I was just about to look there," he said matter-of-factly.

"*Uh-huh.*"

He bent on one knee and covered his mouth; the smell was almost unbearable. Kate thumped his shoulder with a flashlight.

"Where'd that come from?" he asked.

"It was on the counter by the microwave. You should really be more observant."

He clicked it on. "Okay. I'm going in."

"Be careful."

"Careful," he chuckled, flattening himself on the floor and flooding the underside of the fridge with light. "Why the hell would I need to be—"

That was when he saw it: a blob of a shape near the back corner.

"Jesus," he cried, scrambling to his feet. "There is a rat the size of a *squirrel* under there."

Kate drew back a step. "Don't joke."

"Do I look like I'm joking?" He wiped a shaky hand across his mouth. "Not cool. Not cool at all."

"Is it dead?"

He glared at her. "I didn't check for a pulse, but I'm pretty sure they don't make that smell when they're alive."

"What do we do?" she asked. "Call an exterminator?"

"Fifty bucks for fifteen minutes of work? No thanks."

"We can't just leave it there."

"*Obviously*," he replied curtly. "We just need to find a way to get it out. Maybe if we—"

"No way," she said, taking another step back. "There's no *we*. I'm not going near that thing."

"Fine. Then at least help me find something long. Something like . . ."

He looked out the sliding glass door at the charcoal grill on the deck. A set of cooking tongs hung from one side, and he went out and retrieved them.

"That's so wrong," said Kate.

"You got a better idea?"

He lowered himself back to the floor. Nothing about this was going to be pleasant, but he couldn't leave it there, and he wasn't going to pay someone to remove it. He doubted Mortom even had an exterminator.

"Piece of cake," he reassured himself.

The tongs were stiff and awkward in his hands, and the moment they touched the rat his whole body recoiled.

"What? What's wrong?"

"Gloves," he said, covering his mouth with the back of his forearm. "Find me some dishwashing gloves or something."

Kate randomly began opening cupboards. He told himself he could do this; it was just a dead animal. At the age of ten he had buried his cat in the backyard and even kissed its head before placing it in the ground.

But a rat wasn't a cat—not by a long shot. A rat was a disease-carrying, germ-infested, vicious animal with beady eyes.

"There's nothing," she said. "Do you want me to look in the bathroom?"

The gloves were just a stall and he knew it. And the longer he sat there, the harder it was going to be.

"Andy?"

"No," he huffed. His heart was pounding now. "I got this."

He reached underneath with the tongs and closed them around the rat's tail. He gave a tug; nothing happened. He pulled with more force, feeling the coarse, rubbery skin through the wooden handles. The rat shifted and he caught a glimpse of its head. Something was inside its mouth. He pushed himself up from the floor, leaving the tongs where they lay.

"Well?" she asked.

He waited until he was in the dining room before opening his mouth for air. "Stuck. It's wedged tight."

"How could it be stuck? It had to get in there in the first place."

"I saw something in its mouth." He wiped his forehead, removing a few drops of sweat. "I'm guessing it choked to death and bloated."

"So now what?" she asked. "Exterminator again?"

"Kate, I already told you—"

"What's a few bucks? You just inherited a whole house."

"Can you help me pull?"

She narrowed her eyes. "What do you mean?"

"The rat's pretty far in there. Maybe if we pull out the refrigerator we can get to it from the back side."

Kate was shaking her head before he finished. "I can't."

"Look," he said, "all I'm asking is for you to help me move the refrigerator a few feet. Then you can run out of the room shrieking like a girl, okay?"

He expected her to blow up, but she only stared at him with wounded eyes. All the color was gone from her face.

He pushed out a sigh. The only way this rat was coming out was from the front, and if it truly was wedged in there, grilling tongs weren't going to get the job done.

"Is there a kitchen mitt?" he asked.

"Let me look . . ."

He rubbed the sweat from his palms, knowing he wasn't going to be able to do it but knowing he had no choice.

"Here," she said, shoving one at him. It was frayed and burnt in several places, but it was also thick with padding. He wrestled it over his hand and kicked away the tongs.

She said, "I still think we should wait—"

"And I said I got this, okay?"

He lay on his side, reached under the refrigerator, and gripped the tail as tightly as the mitt would allow. The smell was immediately inside his mouth, invading his lungs with each breath.

"Come on," he said through clenched teeth, pulling and praying the tail wasn't going to break off—

And then it was done.

He scrambled to his feet as Kate fled down the hallway. The rat was sideways by the oven, peppered with dried blood and dirt. Inside its mouth was a triangle of folded paper.

"What the hell?"

He knelt beside it. The paper was white with no markings, maybe four inches point to point. There was no question it had been forced into place—the question was why.

There was only one way to find out.

The rat watched with flat, marbled eyes as he worked the triangle free. Something heavy shifted inside the folds.

Slowly, methodically, he began peeling back layers of paper. The object inside dropped to the floor with an audible clink.

It was a locker key.

He stared at it without blinking, trying to make sense of what he was seeing . . . then realized the answer was already in his hands.

He finished unfolding the paper. Written inside were two words:

FOLLOW ME

2

"Is it gone?" Kate hollered from the bathroom.

"Yeah," Andy called back. "I flung it into the backyard. Come on out."

She warily made her way past the kitchen and found him at the dining room table, staring into a bowl.

"What are you looking at?" she asked, not wanting to know.

"The snack our friend was chewing on."

She leaned over the table. It was a key, but not the kind that started cars or opened doors. This key was short and wide with a green head. The number twenty-three was stamped into the plastic.

"It looks like one of the locker keys at my gym," she said.

"Or a key to a locker at an airport terminal. Or shopping mall."

"But why was it with the rat?"

His eyes narrowed as they flicked to hers; it was an expression she knew well.

"What aren't you telling me?" she asked.

"Nothing. It's just . . . it's almost as if someone left it here to be found."

"But who would do something like that? And why wouldn't Craig know there was a dead rat under his refrigerator?"

She looked at him. His hands were wrapped around the bowl, his face pinched in thought. She could almost see the wheels turning.

"Maybe Craig was the one who left it," he said mildly.

There was a knock at the front door. Andy sat motionless, fixated on the key. Kate nudged him with a jolt of impatience.

"Yeah," he said, "I'm going." He stood without taking his eyes from the bowl. "Don't do anything with this."

"What would I do with it?"

"Just don't touch it, okay?"

She scowled as he left, half-tempted to drop it into the sink. And if the garbage disposal accidentally switched on and mangled the key beyond use . . . well, too bad for him.

Instead she went to the staircase and saw Andy shaking hands with a middle-aged man sporting a dark suit.

"I didn't expect to find you inside," Mr. Thatcher was saying. "My suggestion to meet here was only so we could perform a brief walk-through of the property together."

Andy lowered his voice. "Lunch burrito was trying to escape down my leg. It was a photo finish to the toilet."

Thatcher frowned. "Yes. Well. As long as you understand that none of this is legally yours until the estate closes. All personal effects must remain inside the house, untouched."

"Got it." Andy motioned at Kate. "The woman hovering above us is my parents' other child, Katie."

"Just Kate," she said. "And thank you again for meeting us on a Sunday. It was very generous."

"We strive to settle these matters as quickly as possible. Would you prefer to follow me back to my office, or shall I just give you the address?"

"Actually," said Andy, "I was hoping to pop off the paperwork here."

"That would be highly irregular—"

"Oh, we won't tell if you won't. And I'm willing to bet the papers to sign are in the briefcase by your feet. You strike me as the type of man who always comes prepared."

"I do indeed have the documents, but—"

"Then it's settled." Andy gestured at the stairs. "After you, of course."

Thatcher pursed his lips. "Since you seem to insist, I suppose we could make an exception."

They made their way up the staircase. Thatcher sniffed at the air and eyed the hallway suspiciously.

"Maybe the living room would be best?" Kate suggested. "There's a lovely breeze coming through the windows."

Thatcher gave her a perfunctory smile and made his way to the corner chair. Andy sat on the coffee table and clapped his hands. "Let's get this over with."

"Yes," Thatcher said shortly. *"Let's."*

He opened his briefcase and took out a thick manila envelope. Two newspaper articles were neatly clipped to the front.

"Is that the obituary?" Kate asked.

"We like to be thorough with our records."

"May I see it?"

Thatcher hesitated before passing it over. It was a single paragraph with no picture.

Craig Matthew Moore, 33, of Mortom, was pronounced dead on arrival Tuesday, July 3 at Van Duten County Hospital, Keota. He was born September 1, 1974, the son of Mary Louise Moore. Funeral services will be held Friday, July 6 at St. Joseph United Church in Mortom with Rev. Gordon Engel officiating. Burial will be in St. Paul's Cemetery.

"Where is Saint Paul's Cemetery?" Kate asked.

"That would be the west side of town, past the nursing home and near the baseball diamonds."

Andy said, "We passed a cemetery as we came in—"

"That would be the original town cemetery, filled and forgotten years ago."

"Fascinating," said Andy. "And the other clipping attached to your little folder? Is that Craig-related as well?"

Thatcher cleared his throat. "Again, just for our records. We strive to be—"

"Thorough," Andy remarked, taking the clipping. "So you've said."

> MORTOM—The death of a 33-year-old at Lake Smock on Tuesday evening has been ruled a drowning, according to preliminary autopsy results. Craig Moore was found in the lake after apparently falling from a cliff. The investigation was hampered by a lack of witnesses, but Sheriff William Barton stated the autopsy report indicates the death was accidental. "He (Moore) struck rocks on the way down, but the injuries were not fatal," Barton said. "The doctor who performed the autopsy said he was probably unconscious in the water, but the death was from drowning."

"That's one you don't walk away from," Andy said, shaking his head.

Thatcher's eyes dropped to the clipping. Andy held it a moment longer before handing it back, just to be difficult.

"I assure you," Andy said somberly, "it is with a heavy heart and hand that I sign the papers you are about to present to me."

A humorless smile touched Thatcher's lips. "As you know, there was only one stipulation in the will—"

"That I come and visit the house within one week of Craig's death," Andy finished. "Nothing about how long I had to stay, or anything special I had to do . . . only that I had to come and step foot inside. And here I am."

"Sorry to interrupt," said Kate, "but I think I'll let the two of you finish in private. Is there a good restaurant in town, Mr. Thatcher?"

"The Fine Supper Club is *excellent*. It's three blocks east on Maple Street." He consulted his watch. "But I would recommend going now to secure a table. The Fine Supper Club does fill quickly."

"Sounds fine and excellent to me," Andy agreed, tossing his keys at Kate. "Take the truck and I'll walk there when we're done."

Kate forced a smile. "Would you see me out please, Andy?"

"Absolutely." He winked at Thatcher. "Who says family chivalry is dead?"

He followed Kate down the staircase and almost got whacked by the screen door as she slammed it.

"You're being an ass," she said in a hushed voice.

"Goddamn suit," Andy grumbled. "I can't believe—"

"That you used to be one of them? You did. Back when you had a job and a life to boot. Maybe this town and these people are a big joke to you, but try and remember that your actions also reflect badly on Aunt Mary."

"Uh, you do realize you're talking about a woman who moved here pregnant and single at age nineteen, then proceeded to raise a man-boy who lived with her until he was in his mid-twenties. What could I possibly do or say to tarnish *that* groundwork?"

Kate opened her mouth, closed it, and went down the steps without another word. If he wanted to continue to act like an overgrown smart-ass, she would just flat out ignore him.

"Be sure to order me varmint," he called after her. "*Coon* plugs me up!"

She got in the pickup and shut the door hard enough to rattle the rearview mirror. It was official: her brother was a thirty-year-old child. Not that there was ever much doubt.

She closed her eyes and pulled in a deep breath. Two minutes of focused breathing, then she would try to think of one reason to *not* drive back to Luther and leave him stranded—

There was a knock on the glass. Her resolve broke and she whirled in a fit of anger. "Leave me the hell alone!"

The girl standing there took a startled step back. "Sorry."

"Wait," Kate said, fumbling for the door handle. "I didn't mean—"

The girl was already halfway down the street. Now Kate was scaring off the neighborhood kids. Their mother would be proud.

She started the pickup, gave the horizon a final glance, and set out for the restaurant to wait for her brother.

It was turning into a glorious day.

3

"So I basically have two choices," Andy said, shoving a forkful of potatoes into his mouth. "I can keep the house and all the stuff inside, or I can let Thatcher auction it all off and mail me a check. He said the estate shouldn't take more than a couple weeks to close, so I have until then to decide."

Kate lifted her eyes momentarily and dropped them back to her plate. She pushed around her food indifferently.

"Craig had nothing in his savings or checking accounts, so it's only the house we're dealing with. Thatcher thinks he could get around fifty grand for it. Of course, he neglected to tell me the most important part until later. . ." He frowned at her. "Do you want to hear this?"

"Sure," she said absently.

"The fifty grand would be applied toward the mortgage, inheritance tax, property tax, and Thatcher's percentage for being executor. So there would probably be something like thirty thousand dollars left."

"Ah."

"And then we get to the credit card debt," he said with a grimace. "Twenty-five thousand dollars. So if I'm lucky, I'll maybe end up with five grand. Thatcher also said his estimates were optimistic, so in the end there could actually be nothing left. I could pretty much break even."

"How terrible if you couldn't benefit from Craig's death," Kate said testily.

"But here's the funny thing. Craig only drew up his will a few weeks ago, and if not for that, I wouldn't have gotten anything—"

"Andy," she huffed, her fork clanking down onto the plate. "How can you be so cold?"

"All I'm saying is that it's a good thing he left it to *someone*. Otherwise it could have all gone to the state and been lost. At least now Mary has a chance to go through the house and take anything she wants."

"I can see why Craig was so generous toward you. You're such a considerate guy."

"Look, I don't know why Craig left everything to me; I'm just trying to get things in order and do what needs to be done. Can you at least try to understand that?"

"I'm tired and I don't feel good," she said. "I just want to get out of here and find a hotel, okay?"

"You kids need anything else?"

Back in Luther, the waitresses were young and busty. In Mortom, it was a grandmother with a mustache.

"Only for you to give my compliments to the cook," Andy said with a smile. "Let me guess: You have a little old lady in the kitchen whipping up recipes that have been in the family for years, right?"

"I'll tell Harry you enjoyed the instant potatoes," she said, dropping the bill and moving on.

Andy dug out his wallet. "We'll find a place to stay after I fill up the truck."

"Fine. Whatever."

He laid a twenty on the table and brought up the contents of his pockets, looking for change.

"What the hell?" Kate gasped.

He slipped the locker key back into his pocket. "It's nothing."

"*Nothing?*" she echoed incredulously. "Andy, you found that with a dead—"

"Probably not restaurant conversation," he cut in, smiling at the elderly couple two tables over.

"Why in God's name are you carrying it?"

He leaned forward. "There's something I didn't tell you earlier. I also found a piece of paper with the key that said, 'Follow me.' I didn't say anything because I knew you'd be weird about it."

Kate's forehead creased. "Weird about what? Junk you found under the fridge?"

"Don't you get it? The key was left there on purpose. It was left there for me to find."

"You're joking, right? Please tell me you're kidding."

He shook his head. "Just forget it. You're only going to believe what you want, no matter what I tell you. Or show you."

"I'm just trying to understand—"

"There's nothing to understand," he said, sharpening his tone. "The key was wrapped inside a note and shoved into the rat's mouth hard enough to break its jaw loose."

"Andy . . . ," she said sickly.

"Someone did this, Kate. Someone who knew the rat's body would bloat and deteriorate and stink enough to be discovered."

Kate didn't hear; she was stumbling toward the bathroom with one hand clamped over her mouth. Andy leaned back in his chair and caught their waitress staring.

"Be sure to tell Harry my sister especially enjoyed the food," he said.

He took out the key. It didn't matter what Kate believed; he knew the truth. The key was meant to be found, and it was meant to be found by him. Things were in motion that couldn't be changed or stopped.

He didn't know if the thought was exhilarating or terrifying.

4

Andy returned the nozzle to the pump and did a quick check of his cash; the station barely looked modern enough for bathrooms, let alone an ATM or credit card machine. If not for the bright orange "Open" sign in the window, he would have thought the place abandoned. Or condemned.

He crossed the lot and stepped inside. The stool behind the counter was unmanned, and most of the racks and shelves were empty. The place smelled of cigarette smoke and bug spray.

"Hello?" he called out.

He bellied up to the counter and picked up a newspaper. The headline read "Champion Market Steer" and featured a girl holding a blue ribbon. It was dated last Thursday.

"Can't wait to see what's in today's edition," he mused.

"Probably the winner of last week's chili contest."

Andy looked over his shoulder with a start. The man coming through the door was saddled in gray overalls and easily weighed a healthy three hundred. His brow was beaded with sweat and a broad smile filled his face.

"Only one paper for the whole county," the man explained, "and it comes out once a week. Nate Shawler, proprietor of the ground you stand on."

The man held out his hand and Andy shook it without hesitation. A long, saw-toothed scar trailed his forearm, and Andy shifted his gaze when he realized he was staring.

"Beauty, huh?" asked Nate. "A little gift for my contribution to Nam."

"You were in the war?"

Nate laughed as he stepped behind the counter. "I served my country by working in a munitions factory. My second day there some fool knocked over a table and lost a grenade to the floor."

"Exploded?" Andy asked with a grimace.

"Stupid me didn't see it and tripped. I came down hard on the edge of the table and ripped it open. How's *that* for a war thriller?"

Andy chuckled. "Thrilling."

"I'm guessing that's your truck at the pump?"

"Yeah, I pumped forty in gas." He eyed the rack behind the counter and added: "I'll take some cigarettes, too. The cheapest you got."

"Cheap I can do. Buy two packs and I'll throw in an unfinished crossword."

Andy glanced at the open magazine. "Not going so well?"

"Last one has me stumped. I need a five-letter word for 'varnish resin,' and the best I can figure—"

"Elemi."

Nate cocked an eyebrow as he passed over the cigarettes. "Now how in God's name would you know that? I had three letters of it and still couldn't put it together. I even tried looking in the dictionary and couldn't find a thing. And I'll be damned . . . It fits!"

"Puzzle solving is about the only thing I was ever good at."

Nate wrote in the remaining two letters and seemed to stand a bit taller. "I suppose it's cheating, but I won't tell if you won't. Thank you, sir."

"Call me Andy."

"Andy it is. So what brings you to our town, if I might ask?"

"Actually, my cousin just died—"

"I knew it," said Nate, snapping his fingers. "Craig Moore, right? I thought you looked familiar. Not that we've met, but you two look alike—almost close enough to be brothers. Anyone ever tell you that?"

Andy tried to smile but wasn't quite able to. "Not really."

"That's funny about the crosswords, because Craig used to come in and buy all sorts of them. Must run in the family."

"It was about the only thing we had in common."

"You're a little late for the funeral, aren't you? That was last Friday."

Andy hesitated, unsure how to respond. The last thing he wanted to do was explain his business to everyone he met.

"Came down to settle some affairs," he said, leaving it at that. "Did you know Craig very well?"

"Well enough. He came in every Saturday night at five on the dot. He'd fill up that moped of his and then drive off to Keota with a fifty-dollar bill in his hand."

"Fifty-dollar bill?"

"Keota is about twenty miles north of here. Craig always said he was scared of falling asleep while driving, so he figured holding money in his hand would help keep him awake. Don't know how a person could fall asleep while operating a moped, but to each their own. He was a strange one at times."

"I didn't really know him as an adult," Andy confessed. "When we were kids, he would come and stay with us in the summers, but as we got older I mostly only saw him at family reunions."

"What was he like when he was younger?"

"*Cocky.* Every time he won an award he'd mail us the newspaper clipping. My mother still has one from when he won the state spelling bee."

"He was a smart fella," said Nate. "That much was obvious."

Andy shrugged. "I better keep moving. Hey, is there a hotel in town?"

"Closest one is in Keota. They should be able to fix you up."

"Thanks." He took out two twenties. "How much for the cigarettes?"

Nate considered. "Let's call it a condolence offering."

"That's not necessary—"

"Sir, *never* argue with the proprietor of the only gas station in town. It's just not right."

"Didn't I see another station a few blocks over?"

"Let's just say I hope to get all your business while you're visiting. We don't do too much of it around here."

"Fair enough. And thanks again."

"Don't be a stranger," Nate called after him.

Andy tossed a guilty wave over his shoulder, knowing he would probably never see him again. Tomorrow they would be back on the road and Mortom would be no more than a memory.

The sooner, the better.

5

Kate didn't speak until they reached Keota, and that was only to remind him there was no way they were driving back to Luther that night. Andy agreed with a nod—there was no way in *hell* they were driving back. Nate had said that Craig went to Keota every Saturday night, so there was a strong possibility that the key opened a locker somewhere in town. He felt this so strongly that he was barely able to contain himself when he saw the bowling alley across the street from the hotel.

"Hey," he said, "I'm gonna grab a soda while you get the scoop on a room, okay?"

She narrowed her eyes and gave him a *Do you really think I don't know what you're up to?* glare.

"Get something cheap," he told her, climbing out.

He crossed the street in a rush and almost got clipped by a car. His hand tightened around the key. It was a long shot, but he had to start somewhere. And if the key did open a locker and all he found was dirty socks and underwear . . .

There was no reason to speculate; he would find out soon enough.

The bowling alley was deserted except for a handful of teens crowded around a pinball machine. He passed by them without a glance and felt a welt of excitement as he spotted a row of gray lockers along the back wall. His enthusiasm was short-lived, however; the heads of the keys were red, not green, and there was no locker 23.

"Big surprise," he muttered.

He was an idiot if he thought anything about this was going to be easy. Keota was probably a hundred times the size of Mortom. Was he really going to stop at every place he passed that might hold lockers? But what other choice did he have?

He left the alley and found Kate by the truck. She had one hand on her stomach, and her face was flushed.

"You okay?" he asked. "Throw up again?"

"I never threw up at the restaurant," she said. "My stomach is just touchy, kind of like your mouth."

Andy nodded, grateful he was being spoken to again.

"Bad news or good news first?" she asked.

"Why do I have a feeling they both suck?"

"There's a festival going on this week, and the lady said all the hotels within thirty miles are packed. This is the only hotel in Keota, and it only has one room available."

"Let me guess, suite?"

"Presidential."

"How much?" he winced, not wanting to know.

She said, "One hundred—"

"A hundred dollars?"

"And thirty," she finished.

"My God, does it come with a hooker?"

"Or we can keep driving. The lady said we could probably find something in Hapsburg, but that's another thirty miles from here. Andy, I don't think my stomach could take it."

"Fine, but only if the room has two beds. I'm not sleeping on the floor, and I'm not sleeping with you. You snore too much."

"Agreed. I take it you didn't find a locker full of gold?"

"Very funny. And no."

"You get the bags, and don't look to me for conversation tonight. I'm using all the hot water in the shower and then crawling into bed. And if you do bring home a hooker, keep it quick and quiet."

"Yes, ma'am."

He picked up her bag with a grunt. From the weight of it she had easily packed two weeks' worth of clothing.

"Did you want to swing back through Mortom tomorrow before heading home?" he asked. "You never did get a chance to see Mary, and I'm sure you'd like to visit Craig's grave."

She eyed him suspiciously. "That's very considerate of you."

"Anything for my favorite sis," he said with a smile.

And when they were back in Mortom he would take a hard look around the house, just to be sure there was nothing else to be found.

6

Andy tossed away his covers and glared at the clock; it was past two and he wasn't even drowsy. Kate was lying on her stomach with one arm off the bed, and—true to her word—had passed out five minutes after showering.

He took the key from the nightstand and turned it over in his hands. Sleep would be impossible until he figured out what it opened. It was a puzzle, and every puzzle had a solution. All he had to do was take the time to examine the facts.

First and foremost was Craig's will, created shortly before his death and containing the bizarre stipulation about going inside the house within one week. Nothing about how long Andy needed to stay—only that he physically had to go inside. It was obvious the stipulation existed for him to find the rat, but if it had been put there by Craig, didn't that mean Craig knew he was going to die? And if so, didn't that make it suicide?

He shifted uneasily at the thought but didn't push it away. Craig could have easily put the rat there before jumping off the rocks . . . but *why*? If the key was important to find, why risk hiding it? Why not simply leave it in an obvious place? Why put it in the mouth of a dead rat to be found under the fridge? And while he was addressing the issue, where exactly did a person get a rat—

He sat up abruptly, his breath catching in his throat.

"The rat," he whispered. The answer had been in front of him the whole time.

He leapt from the bed and was out the door before his shirt was pulled over his head.

7

He shook the knob again, this time with more force. The front door was locked. And why wouldn't it be? He clearly remembered locking it when they had left earlier that day. There was no reason for it; he had done it out of simple habit. The goddamn house had probably never been locked the whole time Craig lived there, and now Andy had locked himself out.

He made his way into the backyard, mindful of the rat hidden somewhere in the overgrown grass. As long as he stayed close to the house he would be okay, because if he stepped on the rat he would most definitely scream. There was no question.

The steps to the deck groaned under his weight as he cast a furtive glance over his shoulder, feeling like a criminal. If the patio door was locked, he would go back to the hotel and that would be the end of it. He wouldn't try to find another way in, or even go so far as to break a window to get inside. That would be madness.

The door opened easily on its track. Now he had to figure out where to start. It wasn't exactly a needle in a haystack, but he also wasn't sure what he was looking for. He would know when he saw it, though. Of that he was certain.

"Where would you be?" he asked no one in particular.

His gaze fell across the staircase. He hadn't been in the basement yet; that was the place to start. Or the garage. The garage was even better.

He scurried down the staircase and snapped on the light. The main basement was unfinished, but there was a small room to the left with carpet and drywall. Inside sat a twin-sized bed with what looked to be fresh sheets and new pillows.

He lingered for a moment, wondering why Craig would go to the trouble of setting up a guest room, then shrugged it off. It wasn't his primary concern.

The room was immediately forgotten when he opened the door to the garage. Hundreds of empty soda cans covered the floor. More were packed into clear garbage bags and piled onto the workbench; the place looked like a mini–recycling center.

He did a quick search with his eyes, not wanting to step any farther inside than he had to. Not that there was much else to see. A lawnmower with no gas cap, a bicycle with two flat tires, some gardening tools . . .

He closed the door and turned his attention back to the basement. Cardboard boxes were stacked endlessly along the far wall, and he hoped like hell he wasn't going to have to turn them out. There were too many to count and most were taped shut.

"It's here," he assured himself. "Somewhere . . ."

He moved to the center of the room and caught sight of the crawl space under the stairs. A white sheet had been nailed over the opening, and his pulse quickened as he pushed it aside and saw the fish tank on the floor. The glass was streaked and cracked in several places, but this tank hadn't been used for fish—it had been for something else. A thin layer of shredded newspaper covered the bottom, along with two plastic bowls. Both were empty, but he had no doubt they had recently contained food and water. Some people kept dogs; others preferred cats. And if those were too large or messy, there were always things like lizards and rabbits. Or sometimes—just sometimes—people fancied something a little more unique. *Rats make great pets*, one of his coworkers had once told him.

He wet his lips and reached inside the tank. His fingers pawed through the shredding, exploring the bottom and probing the corners. There was nothing.

"It has to be," he croaked.

He lifted the tank and dumped all its contents to the floor. His heart ground to a stop when he saw the envelope taped to the bottom of the tank.

Written across the front was a single word:

ANDREW

MONDAY

8

Kate opened her eyes.

The first thing that came into focus was a pale blue wall that didn't belong in her apartment . . . because she wasn't in her apartment—she was in a hotel room. The events of the last twenty-four hours came back in a rush, and when she lifted her head she let out a startled cry. Andy was staring at her from the floor, a lit cigarette jittering between his fingers.

"What the hell?" she managed. "And why are you smoking again?"

He stabbed it out in the trash can. "I went back to Mortom and found the rat."

Her stomach lurched. "From the backyard?"

"No," he spat. "It was the rat that was the clue, not the key. Here, look at this."

He was holding a piece of paper, and when she didn't take it he tossed it on the bed.

"What is it?" she asked.

"I found it taped to the bottom of the rat cage. Craig had a pet rat . . . Just read it, okay?"

She tentatively picked it up. It looked to be some sort of letter, written in pencil.

"Out loud," he told her. "Read it out loud."

"My cherished cousin," she read. "I theorize one of two things has occurred. You've either stumbled across this letter by chance, or you've worked out the first clue." The sheet dipped in her hand as she looked up. "First clue?"

"Keep reading."

Kate frowned. "I had originally planned to give Annabelle to Debbie as a parting gift, but in the end she was needed more in death than life. And in case you were curious, I drowned her in the toilet. Poetic, don't you agree?"

"It's very simple," Andy said.

"What?"

He pointed at the letter. "That's the next line."

"How many times did you read this?"

"Just wait. It gets better."

Kate hesitated a moment before continuing. "It's very simple. Solve one clue and follow it to the next. And believe me when I say it's in your best interest to succeed, because there is a time line. Hopefully you departed for Mortom posthaste, as you only have until Friday the thirteenth to unravel all the clues. Ironic how the dates worked themselves out, don't you think? Since I perished on a Tuesday—"

Kate dropped the paper like it had caught fire. "What the hell is this?"

"I told you, I found it."

"How could he write this? He didn't know he was going to die."

"Finish the letter," Andy said quietly.

Her face darkened. "I don't know what you're trying to do, but I don't want any part of it."

Andy picked up the sheet. "Since I perished on a Tuesday, you should have an abundance of time, even if you waited to come until the last possible day. I strongly suggest you stay and play. Something unpleasant will transpire if you haven't finished by Friday, regardless of where you are. So really, there is no choice. And with that, I propose one final question: Why are you still squandering time with this letter? Open the other envelope, because the game has already begun."

Andy set the paper down. Kate gaped at him, unsure where to begin.

"He killed himself," Andy said. "This letter proves—"

"*Nothing*. It proves nothing, except that some sicko is playing a sick joke."

"Think about it for a minute. How could Craig know he would die on a Tuesday unless it was planned—"

She opened her mouth and he held out a finger.

"And think about the rat comment. He says he drowned it and it's poetic. Why is that poetic? Because that's what happened to him. Craig not only knew he was going to die on that Tuesday, but also that he was going to die by drowning. He knew all this before he wrote the letter."

"But why . . . There wasn't . . . ." She struggled with her words, processing them in her head but unable to spit them out. "Are you saying he fell off the rocks on purpose?"

"He committed suicide," Andy said. "People do it all the time."

"Not in our family!" Kate cried. All at once she found herself on the verge of hysteria. "And even if he did, why would he kill a rat and tell you to play some game? It's sick and it's wrong. Someone is playing a joke."

"Who? Nobody here knows me. But maybe you're right. Maybe Mary was so pissed that Craig left everything to me that she decided to mess with my head. Should we lay a trap and catch her in the act?"

Kate crossed her arms. "This is the dumbest conversation we've ever had."

"Look," he said, "for the sake of argument, let's put aside *who* left the letter and think about *why* it was left. Somebody wants me to play this game, and I only have until Friday. Four days from now."

"And what do you expect to find?" she asked. "A million dollars?"

"No," he said . . . but she could see in his eyes that he did expect to find something along those lines.

"You're going to do this no matter what I say, aren't you?"

"What if it is something?" he asked. His eyes were glistening. "What if Craig did kill himself? Don't you want to know? If he took his own life, don't you think we owe it to our family to follow this through and see where it leads? Don't we owe it to Craig?"

Kate found herself listening and not liking it. Her brother was as clever with words as he was with puzzles.

"And that's why you want to do this?" she asked. "Out of concern for Craig and our family, and not because you think there's some prize at the end of it all?"

"I just want to know what's going on." There was nothing in his voice as he spoke, making it impossible to read his tone. "If you don't want anything to do with this, I'll drive you home and turn around and come right back. Or we both stay. All I want is a couple days to figure this out. You don't have to do anything."

"And what if we do find out that it was Craig who left the letter? If he did actually take his own . . . you know. Then what do we do with that information?"

"We take it one step at a time. And until then we don't tell anyone, agreed?"

"I don't like this," she said in a tight voice. "I don't like this one bit. But it's stupid to make you take me back home when you'll just turn around . . ."

He was staring at her, his body pitched forward. The other envelope was in his hands, still sealed.

"So open it," she said brusquely.

9

Kate said nothing on the drive back to Mortom. Any other time this would have concerned Andy (Kate was one of those people who couldn't *think* something without saying it), but this time he welcomed the silence. There were greater matters at hand. Namely, the second envelope, which had contained a small index card with three words:

palm the Kreab

There was no such word as *kreab*—of this he was almost positive. He would check a dictionary, just to be safe, but his mind was already working in other directions. Tracking down a state map was a top priority. If Kreab was a nearby city or town, he would find it. Getting his hands on a phone book was also at the top of his list. A last name like Kreab would stick out like a sore thumb. It almost sounded foreign.

"Or it could be the name of a company," he said, unaware he was talking aloud. He had no idea what a company named Kreab would make, but it was worth checking out. Nate would know if such a business existed.

"So what's the grand master plan?" Kate asked, breaking her silence. "Will you just wander around the house and look for *secret* messages?"

"Maybe Kreab is a brand name of something. That would make sense. *Palm* it. Pick it up. It's also curious how it's written on the card."

"What do you mean?"

He fished it from his shirt pocket. "The words are on the back side of the index card—the side without the lines—and written upside down. To read it you have to physically flip the card over."

"It looks so . . . different," Kate said.

He started to ask what she meant, then realized it was the house she was speaking of, not the card. He wheeled the truck into the driveway and killed the motor. The house did look different somehow, almost watchful. Craig was dead, but he was still communicating.

"Did you forget to shut the door last night?" Kate asked.

Andy knit his brow as he stepped out from the truck. The front door was standing open.

"I didn't lock it," he said carefully, "but I'm sure I *shut* it."

"Are you sure?"

There was something in her voice he couldn't discern, but it registered when he saw her face. She was spooked.

"Maybe I did forget," he said. When he had left the house, the door had been closed—he was sure of it. "I'll check it out. You wait here."

"Should we call the police?"

"What?" he laughed. His heart was a steady drum inside his chest. "Be serious."

"There is some bizarre stuff going on around here," she said sharply. "Craig's death, the letter, and now this business with the house."

"There's no *business*," he scoffed. "I probably forgot to shut it. And what would we tell the police? 'Can you please escort me inside my dead cousin's house because I left the door unlocked?'"

He was growing irritated, mostly because she was making him edgy.

Maybe Thatcher had come over that morning, or even Mary. Hell, maybe he hadn't shut the door tightly and it had blown open.

"Besides," he said, finishing his thoughts aloud, "it's the middle of the day. If someone is waiting inside to kill me, I'll yell out and you get the cops. Deal?"

"Not funny."

"Seriously, give me two minutes. If I'm not back by then, call the marines. I'm counting on you."

He hurried up the steps, pulse racing. Had he shut the door? Last night was almost a blur now; he barely remembered the drive back to the hotel. Why did he think he could remember something as simple as closing a door?

"Hello?" he called out, stepping inside. "Anyone in here waiting to kill me?"

No response.

He mounted the staircase. He had told Kate two minutes, and knowing her, she would find a phone and call for reinforcements if he wasn't out by then. He had to be quick.

The kitchen was unchanged, as were the living and dining rooms. He made his way down the hallway and paid a quick glance inside the bathroom. Now he was really feeling stupid, like a latchkey kid coming home from school and checking the house for monsters.

He stuck his head inside Craig's bedroom, meaning to give it no more than a brief sweep, and stopped cold. The bottom dresser drawer was open and the clothes inside were bunched. It hadn't been that way before; he was sure of it. He had done a quick exploration of the upstairs after Thatcher had left, and the dresser was one of the things that had caught his eye. Not the dresser itself, but the framed picture on the wall behind it. The memory of standing in front of the dresser and looking at the picture was very clear, and he was almost positive the drawer had been shut.

"Andy!"

He gave the dresser a final, troubled glance before crossing the hallway into the study. The window above the desk stood half open, and he tried to remember if it been that way before. Next he would be jumping at shadows and checking under the beds.

Kate was perched at the edge of the driveway. She raised her hands: *Well?*

"It's fine," he called down. "No serial killers hiding in the closets."

His eyes fell on the desk as he shut the window. The papers there seemed to be in more disarray than before.

"There's no way you can remember that," he told himself unconvincingly.

Jumpy, that was all. And as for the drawer . . . maybe Mary had been over to look for something. Or maybe Kate had done some exploring of her own.

"It was Kate," he said aloud, this time with more conviction. "She was just being nosy like always."

But he wasn't going to ask her. There was no reason to worry her over nothing.

10

Kreab was nowhere to be found.

The phone book had no offerings and the dictionary confirmed it wasn't a word. Nothing in the house had *Kreab* as a brand name—he had even checked the make and model of the moped in the driveway. It was only the second puzzle and he was already stumped.

"Now what?" Kate asked without much interest.

"We have to be missing something. Probably something that's right in front of our faces."

He sat at the table and stared into the index card. It stared back at him, offering no new information.

"I thought I'd go see Aunt Mary," Kate said.

"So go."

"Will you come with me?"

"Nope."

She sat across from him. He forced himself not to make eye contact, knowing he was probably on the verge of hearing a lecture. At least when it was over she would leave and he would have some peace and quiet to figure things out.

"Andy," she said softly. Her hand fell on his wrist. "Death affects everyone very differently. If you're having difficulty coping—"

"I'm not," he said, pulling away from her touch. "I've never bought into the whole 'blood is thicker than water' theory. Craig was my cousin and I'm sorry he died. But I don't feel a loss. Maybe it would be different if I had known him better or we had been closer, but that's not the case. Does that make me an asshole?"

"I'm just saying you've had a lot happen lately, and I'm worried."

"*You're* worried?"

"Okay, Mom and I are worried. We have been ever since the divorce."

"Not this again."

"Andy, it's been over a month and you still won't talk about it. It's not healthy. Then you go and quit your job . . ."

"Go see Mary," he said. "You do your thing and I'll do mine. Okay?"

She stared at him, her lips set in a thin line.

"I can't concentrate with you watching me, Kate."

She stood and went without a word, but only as far as the kitchen. His patience slipped another notch as she picked up the phone book and began flipping through pages.

He said, "I thought you were leaving."

"I don't know where Mary lives," she snapped. "Can I have two seconds?"

He grabbed the card and marched into the living room. If not for Kate and her stupid distractions, he would have probably figured this out already.

"Palm the Kreab . . ."

Three words, written upside down on the back of an index card. That detail was as important as the words—he was convinced of that now. But what did that do for him? Backward and upside down . . . The only other thing he could think to do was rearrange the words to read 'Kreab the palm,' but that made less sense.

He sat on the couch and tried to clear his head. There was no way this was going to beat him. He was smarter than this, smarter than Craig. The puzzle books on the coffee table proved that much. Any grandma with a pencil and an ounce of brain could figure out ninety-nine-cent riddles.

He leaned forward and snatched one up. It was a collection of word scrambles—possibly the easiest type of puzzle ever created. All you did was unscramble words by moving letters around. He opened it to the first page and saw the word *CLIVEHE*.

"Vehicle," he said peevishly.

He couldn't believe people got paid to come up with this crap. Any idiot could take a word and mix up the letters, forward and backward . . .

"Backward," he whispered.

The book fell from his hands as Kate appeared in the dining room. "I can't find Aunt Mary listed anywhere in the phone book—"

"Written on the back!" Andy exclaimed. He rushed past her and slapped the index card on the table. "How could I be so dumb? It's *backward*. Palm the Kreab . . . It's a word scramble."

He grabbed the pen from her hand and wrote

lamp the break

"Break the lamp," he said.

They both looked at the ceramic lamp in the living room. Kate's words echoed through his head as he approached it: *Will you just wander around the house and look for secret messages?* But it couldn't be that easy; there was no way.

"Look at this," he said, a tremor in his voice.

A section of the porcelain base had been broken and glued back together. It was the sort of thing a person wouldn't notice . . . unless they were searching for it. Now it was the most obvious thing in the world.

"Can you reach the plug?" he asked, slipping off the lampshade. "Unplug it."

Andy wet his lips as Kate handed him the cord. He lifted the base and shook it; something rattled inside.

"What are you going to do?" she asked with a touch of petulance. "Just smash it into a million pieces? Mr. Thatcher said none of this was yours yet."

"It fell and accidentally broke," he said, carrying it down the staircase. The driveway was where he was headed, but he reconsidered at the front door. Neighbors were nosy by nature, and destroying things in the driveway was bound to draw attention.

"Coming to your senses?" Kate asked.

"Garage."

He made it into the basement before remembering the aluminum cans. No room to maneuver there. It was going to have to be the basement floor. It was concrete and bare.

"Now what?" Kate asked. "Find a hammer?"

Andy threw down the lamp. It shattered with an explosion of dust.

"Take it easy," she rasped.

He took a knee, his mind seeing but not processing. In the middle of the shattered remains were—

"Leaves," he stammered. "They're tree leaves."

There were a total of three, curled up like dead spiders on their backs.

"What's that?" she asked, pointing.

It was a piece of metal, no bigger than a matchbook cover. He lifted it out and blew away ceramic dust.

"Don't cut yourself," she cautioned.

"It feels like tin or aluminum." He turned it over in his hands. The number forty was scratched into the other side. There was also an arrow pointing up.

"I don't get it—" Kate began, and the doorbell rang.

They both froze as their eyes locked.

"Should I go?" she asked.

For a moment he didn't know how to answer. If it was Thatcher, he would be hard pressed to think up a lie as to why they were back inside the house.

"I'm going," Kate said.

She disappeared up the stairs. Andy returned his attention to the item in his hand. A piece of tin with the number forty and an arrow pointing up . . .

His eyes fell back to the leaves on the floor. This wasn't a word puzzle; this was something else.

"Hungry?" Kate asked. She was holding a covered glass dish with "WELCOME TO TOWN" written across the foil.

"What is it?" he asked.

"Lunch, apparently. Whoever left it didn't stick around, but it feels like it just came out of the oven."

He carefully picked out the leaves. Later he would find a broom to clean up the mess, but only after sifting through the shards, just to make sure nothing else was there.

"Okay," he told Kate.

"Okay what?"

He smiled. "Let's eat."

11

The first bite was toxic. The second bite made her nauseous. When Kate finally put down her fork, she was fairly certain she was in the first stages of diarrhea. The good news was she could throw up over the side of the deck if necessary. Andy was staring at his new find while absently shoveling the casserole into his mouth.

"How can you eat this?" she asked.

He stopped and blinked at his plate. "What is it, anyway?"

"Tuna, I think. I can see why the person left it anonymously."

He shrugged and continued to eat. She felt a stab of anger toward him; he was in full obsession mode now, barely aware of anything around him.

"It has something to do with a tree," he said. "That much is obvious."

"And the tin with the number forty?"

"It could be from a metal sign nailed into a tree somewhere. Or maybe it's telling me that something is buried in a metal box under a tree."

"Forty feet? And why does the arrow point *up*, then?"

"I don't know," he said crossly. "I might be able to figure it out if you'd stop bothering me. I thought you were going to visit Mary."

"You're right. I don't know why I'm wasting my time here with you. Some of us have lives to live. Would it be too much to ask to borrow your pickup again, or should I just storm off on foot?"

He tossed the keys on the table. She snatched them up and cut through the dining room to the staircase.

"Give my love," he called after her.

She flipped him off over her shoulder, not caring if he saw. He had his reasons for staying in town, and she had hers. As long as she remembered that, things would be fine.

She started the pickup and purposely revved the engine before backing out in a burst. It stalled in the street, and her fingers tightened around the wheel.

"Don't let him do this to you, Kate."

She drew in a ragged breath and keyed the engine back to life. Her foot stayed on the brake pedal. She was in no mood to see anyone now, thanks to Andy.

"Asshole."

She sped off down the road, unsure of where she was headed or how far she wanted to venture. The last thing she wanted was to get lost. That was probably impossible in Mortom, but her sense of direction was as lousy as her brother's tact.

"And what have we here?" she asked with a hint of smile.

Two small boys were standing on the sidewalk ahead, giggling and waving in her direction. She slowed the pickup, and they took off running and laughing. One of them hid behind a tree and blew kisses as she passed.

"I seeeeeeee you," she said, pointing a playful finger out the window as she turned the corner.

Her newfound gaiety dried up when she saw the cemetery. It sat on the far side of the road next to a pair of baseball diamonds and was easily three times larger than the cemetery they had passed coming into town.

She brought the pickup to a stop at the entrance and cut the motor. In the distance she could see a man weaving through the headstones, undoubtedly on his way to pay respects to a parent or spouse. Which was exactly what she and Andy should have done the moment they arrived in Mortom: paid their respects.

She stepped out from the pickup, shielding away the sun with one hand. Cemeteries never bothered her (*Safest place to be because everyone is dead*, her father was fond of saying), but she realized her heart was beating quickly. Somewhere inside this cemetery was Craig, who had stayed at their house and eaten at their table. He had been thirty-three, only a year older than she was. He hadn't been sick or old. He had been a young man with a whole life ahead of him. The last time she had seen Craig . . .

She frowned, realizing she couldn't remember. The family reunions had stopped almost a decade ago, but surely she had seen him after that. Her parents came to Mortom at least twice a year, and she always promised herself she would tag along at some point. There would be plenty of time—always a chance to come down and see Aunt Mary and Cousin Craig.

A cool breeze tickled her arms and she shivered. More than anything she wanted to get back in the pickup and leave. She would find Mary, console her, and fervently apologize for missing the funeral.

That was what she wanted to do.

What she was *going* to do was find Craig's grave and pay her respects. Five minutes of her life was all it would take . . . assuming she could find where he was buried. Of course, if the headstone wasn't in place, all she had to do was look for fresh dirt . . .

The thought made her ill as she passed through the open gates. Her eyes touched each headstone as she walked, taking in names and dates. The graves stretched endlessly over the rolling hills—there had to be hundreds. Even if she did manage to find the plot, what then? Say a prayer? Stare pensively at the dirt until she felt she had done right?

She pushed out a frustrated sigh and cupped a hand over her eyes. There was a red pickup parked over the next ridge, and the man she had spotted earlier was loading tools into its bed. Not a visitor after all, but some sort of groundskeeper. If he couldn't help her, no one could.

She started down the hill and stopped when the man let out an inarticulate shout. Her first thought was that he was yelling at her—maybe trying to warn her of something—but his gaze was locked on the ground.

She took a few steps forward, trying to see past the bed of the pickup, and jumped when he shouted again. Only his upper half was visible, but she was able to clearly see him raise the shovel and slam it into the ground. His breath came in loud, short gasps as he brought the shovel up and down, over and over again.

She ducked behind a mausoleum as her mind tried to process the situation. Nothing was forthcoming, and she told herself that whatever this was, she didn't want any part of it. If the guy hadn't noticed her walking up, then he probably wouldn't notice her walking away.

She peered around the edge of the mausoleum. He was by the front of the pickup now, and she told herself to make a break for it. No sooner had the thought left her mind than he snapped his head in her direction.

She jerked back and mentally cursed herself. Why had she looked again instead of just walking off? Now it looked like she was spying. Which, in a way, she kind of *had* been, but seeing someone attack the ground with a garden tool wasn't exactly commonplace behavior. Now she didn't know what to do. If she stayed there, it would look like she was hiding, but if she ran off, it would look even worse.

The seconds passed. She told herself he probably hadn't seen her. He was probably loading his tools and figuring out his next chore . . .

Or sneaking up on her with the shovel.

Her heart shuddered inside her chest. She fought the urge to look again and told herself she was being stupid. The man was a groundskeeper, not some crazed killer. For all she knew he had been beating down a piece of sod or trying to knock out part of a tree stump. Or maybe the guy was having a horrible day and letting off steam. Whatever the case, any minute now he was going to drive off and that would be the end of it—

An engine roared to life. She leaned forward and watched the pickup as it disappeared through the gates on the far side of the cemetery.

"Crazed killer," she scolded herself. "*Stupid.*"

She came out from behind the mausoleum and saw broken dirt where the pickup had been parked. It was unmistakably a grave, but no headstone was in place—only a metal marker.

Her feet moved her forward, slowly at first, then with purpose. Her pulse quickened as she stopped shy of the dirt. The marker was crimped in multiple places, stank of ammonia, and contained three words:

"Craig Matthew Moore."

12

The sound from the kitchen was so unexpected that it actually took Andy a moment to process what he was hearing: Craig was dead (the whole town had to have known this by now), and only a handful of people knew he and Kate were in Mortom, let alone inside Craig's house. A ringing phone was the last thing he expected to hear.

"Wrong number," he mumbled, but a morbid thought crossed his mind: What if it was for Craig? Some old friend calling out of the blue to say hello and catch up on old times. Whatever the case, he sure as hell wasn't going to answer it.

He returned his focus to the leaves. Three of them, curled and brown, impossible to tell what type of tree they had dropped from. Undoubtedly, that would be a part of the puzzle. If they were indigenous to a certain part of the world, he had no clue how he was going to get that information—

"Come on!" he shouted at the phone. It was still ringing: short, intrusive bursts of sound.

He took in a deep breath, his concentration completely broken. The phone was easily on its sixth ring now . . . seventh . . . eighth . . .

He stormed into the kitchen and snared the receiver from the wall. "What?"

There was no response.

"*Hello?*"

His brow furrowed. Someone had called the wrong number, and now they were too embarrassed to speak. And what would they do next? Hang up and immediately call back.

"No one lives here," he said, and started to hang up. A voice on the other end spoke up, and Andy caught the last word: "—there."

He fumbled the receiver back to his ear. "What?"

"So you are there."

"Who is this?"

At first there was nothing, then a small laugh.

"Who are you calling for?" Andy asked, trying to keep his voice steady. "No one lives here anymore—"

"Be seeing ya."

There was a click. Andy held the phone a moment longer before returning it to the wall. Wrong number, that was all. Some guy calling his buddy without realizing he had misdialed. Mortom probably had only one prefix, and it would be easy enough to make that mistake.

He went to the living room window. The street below was deserted—no mysterious men in trench coats staring up at him from a corner phone booth.

"Stop being paranoid," he told himself.

But deep down he knew he wasn't being paranoid—not by a long shot. Things had been anything but normal since arriving in Mortom, and that phone call stank worse than the rat.

He started back toward the deck and jumped when the phone rang again.

This time, he let it ring.

13

Kate stormed up the staircase, snatched the receiver from the wall, and punched out zero for the operator. There was no dial tone. She slammed it down and found Andy on the deck, staring at the tin.

"What's wrong with the phone?" she huffed.

He lifted his head. "When did you get back?"

"Forget it," she said in disgust.

She made her way back outside. He wasn't going to be any help, and Craig's house wasn't the only place with a phone.

She marched across the street and rang the bell twice.

"Come on," she muttered, looking over her shoulder. Andy was standing in Craig's driveway with a stupid look on his stupid face. And he still had the goddamn piece of tin in his hand—

"Yes?"

Kate turned and immediately flushed; it was the girl who had knocked on the pickup window. The girl she had snapped at.

"I'm so sorry for yesterday," Kate stammered. "I thought you were someone else."

"Guess you don't like that person much, huh?"

For a second Kate wasn't sure how to answer. "It's . . . complicated. I need a favor. Can I use your phone to call the sheriff?"

The girl stepped halfway out. "Was there an accident or something?"

"No, I . . ." Kate forced herself to take a breath. "I'm sorry. I was just at the cemetery, and there was a man . . . He was *beating* Craig Moore's grave. And it smelled like he'd urinated on it."

"Was he wearing a camouflage hunting jacket?"

Kate opened her mouth but nothing came out. What difference did it make what the guy was wearing?

"It was probably my grandpa, Ricky," the girl said quietly. "He and Craig had some issues."

"*Issues*," Kate repeated, raising her eyebrows. "Uh, maybe I should speak to your parents."

"You could, but they live in Keota. I stay here with my grandpa a few weeks during the summer."

Kate shrugged back a step. "This is *his* house? Your grandpa?"

"Yeah. My folks started making me come after Grandma died. They won't admit it, but I think it's because they feel guilty that they never want to come visit. Real fair, huh?"

Kate found herself at a loss; she had come over to report an incident, not get sidetracked into a conversation.

"I've seen you and your husband at Craig's house," the girl said. "Are you the new owners?"

"No, we're just here to . . . well, sell it, basically—"

"So you're real estate agents?"

Kate gave a sigh of resignation. "Let's start over. I'm Kate, and the guy is my brother, Andy. Craig was our cousin. When he died, he left his house to Andy. We came to take care of some things, and then we'll go back home."

"I don't blame you for not wanting to stay. There's nothing to do here." The girl dropped her eyes. "And it's lonely with Craig gone."

Kate's brow softened. "Did you know Craig well?"

"Sometimes we would sit on his deck and read together," the girl said vaguely. "We both really liked books. Sometimes he'd read out loud and we'd laugh together at his funny-sounding voice . . . I better go back inside now."

"Okay," Kate said, a bit apprehensively. The abrupt end of the conversation was almost as unsettling as the idea of Craig befriending a girl who couldn't be more than thirteen.

"Can I ask your name?" Kate asked.

The girl hesitated. "Debbie Simms."

"Debbie." Kate gave her a pained smile. "It's nice to meet you."

"I'm sorry my grandpa did that. He doesn't mean it. He just doesn't know . . ."

"Know what?"

Debbie was quiet for so long that Kate thought she hadn't heard the question. "Debbie, what doesn't he know?"

"Everyone in town thinks my grandpa is—" she lowered her voice "—an A-hole, but he's not. He's just looking out for me. I shouldn't have said anything. You should go."

The screen door began to close, and Kate stopped it with her hand.

"I'm sorry, I just . . ." Kate shook her head, trying to sort her thoughts. "I'm just trying to understand—"

"Did you like the casserole?"

Kate fought back a grimace. "That was from you?"

"Did you like it?"

"Um, it was . . ."

"Awful," Debbie answered. "Casseroles are the only thing I learned to make in cooking class, and they never turn out right. But you know what? Grandpa still eats them. He eats them, and he doesn't complain, and it's because we're family. We look out for each other. Okay?"

Debbie shut the door. Kate lingered for a moment before slinking back across the street. Andy was sitting on the hood of the pickup with his head tilted quizzically to one side.

"Care to share?" he asked.

She met his eyes, trying to decide if he was being sincere or sarcastic. It would be easy enough to tell him what had occurred at the cemetery—or that she had just met the Debbie mentioned in the letter—but what was the point? The last thing Andy needed was more ammunition for his stupid cause. Games and puzzles didn't concern her, but family matters did. She had her own agenda now. If something had happened between Debbie's grandpa and Craig, there was only one person in town she could talk to about it.

"I'm taking the pickup to go see Aunt Mary," she said.

"I'll go with."

"Why?" It slipped out more sharply than intended, and she quickly realized she didn't care. She had every reason to be suspicious of his intentions. "Why would you want to do that?"

He smiled. "I can be civil for a short visit. As long as she doesn't pinch my cheeks like she used to."

She studied him, aware he had avoided the question, but knowing the point was moot. If they didn't go together, he would probably just go on his own. Maybe not right then, but at some point. If they went together, she could at least keep an eye on him.

"Fine," she said flatly. "Are you ready?"

He opened the passenger-side door. "Ladies first."

14

In the city of Luther, asking for directions was essentially like begging for change: most people either ignored the request or simply shook their heads before hurrying off. In the town of Mortom, the locals did everything but draw a map.

"Go a mile down the road past an old brick building," the passerby told them. "Then hang a left onto Harrier—that's the street right after Dover—and go two blocks. Then you'll pass a white fence that looks like it was knocked down by a drunken fool in a pickup truck. You can thank Jim Gimbal for that. Keep going straight and you'll see the town dump. Mary Moore has the little brown house next to it. No driveway, but you can park in the street."

Andy and Kate found the house without difficulty, but the place wasn't only next to the dump; it was practically an extension. Mary's lawn looked like a garage sale gone wrong. Metal chairs, a knocked-over charcoal grill, a screen door filled with holes . . . The inventory went on and on, as if Mary's pastime was walking through the dump and collecting items to display in her yard.

"This is nice," said Andy.

"If you're just going to be a jerk—"

"Sorry." He opened the truck door. "Ready?"

"You didn't come here to be sociable or pay respects. You came here to pry, didn't you?"

She watched in contempt as he held up the piece of tin.

"Don't even think about it," she warned. "I did not bring you with me so you could badger Aunt Mary about this stupid nonsense."

"Mary knows the town and the people. I'm not going to say anything about the letter or what's been going on . . . I just want to feel her out and see what she talks about. Probably nothing, but then again . . ."

Kate glared at him. "Then again *what*?"

"At this point I'm not ruling out anything, even that Mary could be involved."

"This is insanity," Kate cried, tossing up her hands. "You don't quit, do you? Maybe I'm the one that wrote the letter; did you ever think of that? Maybe I'm the one doing this, just to mess with your head. Or maybe it's—"

She cut it short, biting back the words.

"It's *what*?" Andy asked.

"Maybe . . . it's someone Craig was dating."

"Kate, you're the worst liar in the world. Who were you going to say?"

"*No one*," she said roughly. She wasn't going to get Debbie involved, no matter what. She reached for the door handle, and Andy grabbed her arm.

"Look," he said, "I wasn't going to say anything because I didn't want to freak you out . . ."

"Freak me out about what?"

"The reason the phone at Craig's house doesn't work is because I unplugged it. Some guy kept calling. Now I wish I had answered it. It could have something to do with all this."

She was shaking her head before he had finished. He was trying to suck her in again—telling stories that had nothing to do with anything.

"I am going to see our aunt," she said. "I'm done with this."

"Fine. I'm sure Mary will be more than happy to tell me what I need to know. And maybe she would be interested in the letter after all. Maybe she'd like to know we think Craig may have offed himself."

"My God," Kate whispered. "How can you be so heartless?"

"Hey, you're the one who thinks it wasn't Craig who wrote that letter. And that means it was someone else—someone who knows things about me. The bottom line is that this *is* happening, and it's happening to me. Do you understand that, Kate? It is happening, and I will do whatever it takes—"

Kate kicked open her door and left him behind, not wanting to hear any more. She was there for Aunt Mary, not him, and she wasn't going to waste any more time listening to his nonsense.

"Four days," he shouted. "Four days and this will all be done."

Her stomach did a slow, forward roll as she stepped onto the porch, and she covered her mouth with the back of her hand.

"Hey," Andy said, coming up behind her. "Are you okay?"

She knocked on the door and winced as her insides shifted again. "Just leave me alone."

"I'm only trying to help."

"I don't . . . I don't need . . ."

She stumbled to the side of the porch and locked her hands on to the railing. She closed her eyes, trying to will her stomach back down.

The front door banged open. "Who's there?"

It came up all at once, showering the side of the porch and the yard.

"Jesus H. Christ, if you wanted to ruin my flowers, you done it," said Aunt Mary.

15

Andy sat quietly at the kitchen table, wondering again how this woman could be related to his mother. Mary stood five feet, weighed somewhere in the ballpark of two hundred, and carried all the personality and charm of a cardboard box. A grunt escaped her mouth as she lifted an oversized can of beans from the cupboard.

"It's rude to stare," she said curtly.

He dropped his eyes. "Sorry."

"Kate gonna be okay?"

"Just an upset stomach," he said, looking over his shoulder. She was still in the bathroom, and there were a few things he wanted to get out in the open before she returned. "We've had an interesting day."

Mary began cranking on the can with an opener, eyes on him. "Figured you'd be in town. Didn't know Kate was coming. Should have called before you come over. I would have cleaned up the house some."

"We would have called, but you aren't in the phone book. That's sort of odd, don't you think?"

"Never been in there. Called once to ask about it. The phone people said it was a mistake and they'd fix it. Never did, but it's just as well. I like my privacy."

"Still, that's part of the service you pay for. You should get it fixed."

"No one calls but your mother. She knows the number."

"Still—"

"You'll have to suffer with the onions," Mary said stiffly, which meant the subject was closed. The beans went into an aluminum pot on the stove. "You never did like onions. Well, these come with them already inside, and I ain't picking them out."

"We didn't come here to eat."

"Always have food for kith and kin. Lots of folks been coming by and bringing food. Funny how when a person dies, folks seem to think the living needs to be fed. Funny how most people also come to the funeral."

Andy mustered a polite smile.

"But I know you been busy," she said. "I hear your wife got your house and you went to an apartment. Shame. Should have treated her better and maybe she would have stuck around."

"Yeah," he agreed, "it's funny about divorces and courts and wills and such."

Mary took a bag of cocktail wieners from the refrigerator and emptied it into the pot.

"Have you been to the house?" he asked. "It looks like someone came over and cleaned out the fridge. I just wanted to thank you if you were the one."

Now he was going to catch her. If she said she had been to the house, he would ask her about the smell. If she played dumb, it was because she was the one who had put the rat there.

"I surely did *not*," she replied sourly. "Craig never was one to grocery shop, especially for perishables. Most times he just ate his meals down at the café. Course, he used to eat here a lot as well. But not much before he died."

"Why's that?" Andy ventured.

Kate appeared in the doorway, her face pale and splotchy.

"There you are," Mary said with a smile. "All better?"

"A little, I think."

"Let's get some food in you and see what it does. I got some left-over tuna salad from last week in the fridge. Got a powerful smell to it, but it should still be good. The key ingredient is fresh pickle juice."

Kate's face lost more color. "I think I'm going to go lie down."

Mary shook her head as Kate staggered out of the kitchen. "Poor thing. And that davenport of mine ain't very kind to lie on. Craig always said he was going to let me have that one of his in the basement, but he never got around to getting it over here."

"You can have it," Andy said in a low voice. He did a quick check over his shoulder, hoping Kate was out of earshot. "If he wanted you to have it, I'll make sure you get it when the legal stuff is all finalized. I just can't understand why he didn't leave it all to you anyway. Doesn't make any sense why he left it to me. Why do you think he would have done that?"

A cold smile surfaced on Mary's lips. "Funny, I was going to ask you the same thing."

They stared at each other. Andy dropped his eyes, not wanting to get into a war of wills. He needed to keep the conversation moving and as relaxed as possible.

"Fetch the plates and silverware from that cupboard behind you," she told him. "Next to the radar range."

He went to it and found paper plates and plastic forks. "I don't see anything but this stuff—"

"Gave up on real dishware long ago. It's easier to just throw stuff away. Usually I just walk to the fence and drop it over into the dump. Billy don't care."

"Billy?"

"Runs the dump."

Andy said lightly, "This wouldn't be a boyfriend of yours now, would it? Come on, you can level with me. Got any new men in your life that no one knows about?"

Mary banged the pot of beans down on the table. "No man in his right mind would come around this place sniffing for the likes of me. What kind of a question is that?"

"Just curious."

"You're curious about some funny stuff," she said, taking the chair across from him. "Now bow your head."

He did as he was told.

"Lord, please bless this food even though you don't seem to bless this family. Amen."

She snapped her fingers for his plate. He held it out as she spooned a mess of beans and wieners across it.

"What about Craig?" he asked. "Did he have a girlfriend named Debbie by chance?"

"Nope."

"How are his friends taking it? I imagine living here for so long he had quite a few of them."

"Craig kept to himself," Mary answered shortly.

Andy stabbed at his beans, growing frustrated. Any second now she would tell him it was rude to talk at the table, and that would end the conversation completely. On his mother's side of the family, supper was for eating and nothing more.

"Surely Craig had friends at work," he pushed, trying to keep his voice casual. "Did he work here in town? I heard he drove to Keota a lot."

"He worked at the graveyard with Ricky Simms."

Andy felt his stomach kick. "Ricky Simms? Was he a good friend?"

She gave a noncommittal grunt.

"Does Ricky live in town?"

"Across the street from Craig's house. Can't get any more in town than that."

Andy leaned forward and lowered his voice. "I think I saw a young girl over there . . . Is Ricky her dad or something?"

"Granddad," Mary replied after a short pause. "Why are you so interested?"

"I just . . ." His palms were sweating and he fought the urge to wipe them. "Someone left a casserole on Craig's front step, and I was wondering if it might have been them."

It was a horrible lie and he knew he was sunk. To his surprise Mary dropped her stare and continued to eat.

"Ricky Simms is not the most pleasant man I have known, but Craig took a strong liking to him. Like I said, Craig worked with him until a few weeks ago, and after that he just did his cans."

"Cans?"

"One of the things he did in Keota. He'd drive around on that moped of his, fishing aluminum cans out from trash barrels. Strange hobby if you ask me. He'd keep them in his garage and return them every Friday. I never understood it."

The fork slipped from Andy's fingers. Cans. Aluminum cans in the garage. *Tin.*

"I have to go," he said, almost knocking over his chair as he stood. "Can you tell Kate I'll be back?"

He was out the door before giving Aunt Mary a chance to respond.

16

Kate awoke with a start, her mind dazed and sluggish. A dull ache invaded her lower back as she stood, and it felt like someone had driven a knife between her shoulder blades. The last thing she remembered was hearing Aunt Mary and Andy talking in the kitchen . . .

"Eight o'clock?" she whispered incredulously, looking at her watch. But it couldn't be that late. She had just closed her eyes a moment ago.

She wandered through the empty kitchen and stepped out onto the porch. Mary was propped up in a lawn chair, effortlessly working a cross-stitch.

"I was wondering if you were going to sleep all evening," Mary said. "You must have been feeling something awful. I can't even fall asleep on that davenport. Springs poke my back too much."

"I'm so sorry. How long was I asleep?"

"'Bout an hour now. Andy still isn't back yet."

Kate's mouth dropped. "He left?"

"Like the devil was on his tail."

"He shouldn't have done that. You should have woken me up."

"Nonsense," Mary said, flapping a hand at her. "You're more than welcome to stay here as long as you like."

"He really hasn't been the same since the divorce," Kate apologized. She was going to slaughter him when he returned. "He isn't always—"

"Evening, Susan," Mary said, raising a hand. The woman strolling past quickened her step without returning the wave.

"Pregnant Suzie Parker," Mary said from the corner of her mouth. "Every night after supper she goes on a walk. Tells her husband it's for exercise and good for the baby. Once she gets around the corner she'll light a cigarette and smoke it to the butt."

"That's terrible," Kate said.

"Most folks think her husband don't know, but I wouldn't bet on it. You can't cover up that thirdhand smoke."

"Thirdhand smoke?"

"That's what Craig always called it. The smoke that gets in your clothes and hair and sticks to your carpet and walls. You can always tell a smoker by their smell."

Kate turned away, slightly embarrassed. She probably had it on her, thanks to Andy.

"But I got no reason to talk," Mary confessed. "Everybody's got their own quirks and secrets. The smaller the town, the harder it is to keep things private. You'd think it'd be easier, but it ain't." She laughed. "I'm probably the only person in the world that ever moved *from* Keota to Mortom. Most folk move from here to there. I supposed I could always go back, but small-town life gets its claws in you and won't let go. I suspect I'll die here myself."

Kate said nothing, trying to read Mary's face. More than anything she wanted to breach the subject of Craig's death but wasn't sure if that had been an opening.

"See that yellow house down across the street?" Mary asked. "Ron and Nelly Pearson. She married Ron after her first husband died. Nelly already had a son, and Ron decided he didn't like the boy's name. He talked her into doing a name change on the boy. Not the last name, but the first name. Changed it from Randy to Cole."

"That's sort of odd. How old is the boy?"

"Twelve."

"Is that even legal?"

"Name change at the courthouse in Keota, eighty dollars. It can be done with parental consent. It's a shame. A real . . ."

Mary was hunched forward, staring off in the other direction. A small sound escaped her lips.

"Aunt Mary?"

"I told myself I wouldn't cry no more."

Kate reached out and touched Mary's shoulder.

"The last time I saw Craig was a week before he died," Mary said vacantly. "He came over and mowed my grass and cleaned out my gutters. We hadn't been talking very much. He was angry with me."

"Angry?"

Mary straightened up. "I suppose that's why he left everything to Andy. He was mad at me and had no one else to give it to. But I didn't care about it. All I wanted was my son not to be upset with me before . . ."

"Before what?"

"I knew," Mary gasped. Her eyes shone as she spoke. "I knew he was going to die."

Kate's pulse kicked up. "It was an accident. There was no way to know—"

"But I did. Kate, I *did* know. And so did he. He had a brain tumor."

At first Kate thought Mary was confused. She was still speaking about one of the neighbors. *Had* to be speaking of a neighbor.

"Who had a tumor?" Kate asked carefully.

"They found it near the back, a small growth. There was nothing they could do. The headaches were so bad that sometimes Craig would sit in a dark room and moan and pray for it all to be over. Craig had no tolerance for pain. Never broke a bone, never had stitches, never twisted or sprained anything in his whole life. I tell myself it was just as well . . . It was just as well that he went . . ."

Kate found herself unable to speak. Craig had been diagnosed with an inoperable brain tumor. He knew he was going to die.

"We told nobody," Mary said, her voice low. "No one knew but him and me and the doctor. Craig wanted it that way. I don't know why I told you now, except . . ."

Dread rose inside her. Now Mary was going to tell her that Craig had committed suicide. Andy had been right all along. Craig had known he was going to die and had taken his own life. She wanted to throw up again.

"You don't have to say it," Kate said gently. "We can't know for sure that Craig took his own life."

"*What?*"

Kate flinched at the sharpness of Mary's voice.

"What did you just say?" Mary rasped.

"I thought . . . wasn't that what you were . . ." Her hands fumbled through the air, trying to cajole the words from her mouth. "Mary, I—"

"How dare you? How dare you sit on my porch and say such wicked things?"

They both turned as Andy's pickup rolled to a stop by the curb. Mary shot him an angry glance before storming into the house.

"What happened?" Andy hollered.

Kate rushed the pickup. "You're an asshole," she spat out. "*That's* what happened."

"What did I do now?"

"Do you know what I was doing while you were off playing your stupid game? Learning our cousin had a brain tumor."

"Shit, are you for real?"

Kate's defenses jumped to full alert. "Why?"

"I found this at the house," Andy said, holding up a postcard. "It's a registration card for a toaster he filled out but obviously never mailed."

"What in God's name—"

"It matches the handwriting from the letter. It proves Craig is the one who did this. He knew he was going to die from this tumor so he committed suicide, but not before setting up this game."

"I just told you Craig had a brain tumor," Kate said, her voice wavering. "Doesn't that mean *anything* to you?"

Andy shrugged. "He's dead. Why should that change anything?"

Kate swung her head toward the house, tears prickling her eyes. She had come to Mortom to comfort and console Mary and had only made things worse.

"Just take me back to the hotel."

"Um . . ."

She whirled on him, ready to pounce. "*What?*"

"I called when I was back at the house, figuring you'd want to stay overnight again. The front desk said another couple grabbed our room right after we checked out, so . . ."

He didn't finish and she didn't need him to. They had two choices: drive back to Luther or stay somewhere else. And there was only one place to stay—only one place they had access to. The idea revolted her, but there was no way she could leave with so much unresolved.

"Drive me to Craig's," she said. "And don't speak to me again today."

He started down the road, and for the first time in her adult life, Kate found herself wishing her brother had never been born.

17

It was almost midnight when the knock came at Kate's door. She rolled over and faced the wall. The downstairs was cold and the bed was lumpy, but it was better than being upstairs with him. In the last forty-eight hours they had alienated their aunt, argued more than they had in their entire lives, and taken up residence in their dead cousin's house. Not only was it creepy being there, but it was also disrespectful and wrong.

The door opened and a sliver of light crept into the room. "You awake?"

She said nothing, although she knew she would. He would talk and apologize and she would soften and start to feel guilty. Fighting had never been one of her strong suits—Andy had gotten all the talent in that department.

The bed groaned as he sat on the edge. "I've never had anyone die on me," he said quietly. "I mean, Mom and Dad are alive, our grand-parents are still here . . . Part of me just doesn't know how to behave. It's almost like it's not real. Maybe if Craig had been someone in my everyday life, it would feel like a loss. But I hardly knew him. And the more I find out . . ."

She lifted her head to see him. His face was no more than a shadow, and she snapped on the lamp by the bed.

"The more I find out," he repeated solemnly, "the more I wonder if I *want* to be sad."

He held up a photograph of him and Craig. At least, she thought it was Andy. Someone had burnt a hole in the picture where his face had been.

"Yeah," he said, "that's me. I found it in Craig's desk. Mary must have taken this at one of the reunions. Nice picture, huh? Looks like someone took a lit cigarette to my head. And Craig didn't smoke."

"Asthma," Kate said vaguely. "I remember him carrying an inhaler. Mom always told you to go outside to smoke so you wouldn't bother him."

"Whatever the case, this isn't the sort of thing that makes a person feel good. Craig did this, Kate. I assure you."

She didn't know what to believe anymore, but she wasn't about to commit to anything. Not yet. He was overlooking the obvious fact that someone else could have written and planted the postcard in an attempt to mislead. And the photograph backed this up as well. Since Craig didn't smoke, didn't that mean someone else had been in the house?

She looked at him, wanting to say these things but not letting herself. Arguing was the first step toward getting involved, and she wasn't going to allow that to happen anymore.

"There's more," he said. "At first I wasn't sure if I wanted to show you, but I think I better." He drew a folded sheet of paper from his shirt pocket. "I found this along with the photo."

She took it from him. "Andrew Christopher Crowl" was written at the top of the page. Below that was Andy's address in Luther, his phone number, birth date, and the license plate number of his pickup.

"What the hell?"

Her eyes moved down. Their parents' names and personal information was next. An icy finger touched her spine when she saw her name at the bottom of the page. The address of her school was also written there.

"What is this?" she asked in a shaky voice. "My phone number isn't even listed in the phone book."

"It's the same handwriting as the letter and the postcard."

She looked at the paper again, trying to rationalize what was there. Addresses . . . phone numbers . . . all *personal* information, but not exactly *confidential* information. All of it could have easily been obtained by anyone who knew the family.

"Whatever it means," he said, "I have less than four days to figure it out."

"Maybe Craig was updating his address book."

"With our license plate numbers?"

She dropped the paper, not wanting to touch it anymore. "I don't know. Maybe he was doing genealogy or something."

"Well, he's pretty damn thorough, then. Why won't you just accept—"

"Accept what? Andy, have you ever stopped to think this is all a bad joke? What if someone is doing this for a laugh or to scare you away for some reason?"

"It says by next Friday—"

"If you want to know the truth, I don't think anything will happen on Friday. Whether you're here or in Luther, nothing is going to happen."

"But how do we know? What if this is real and something does happen? Why would I want to take a chance like that? Why would you? How can you ignore what's staring you in the face?"

The only thing she saw was an overgrown child playing detective. She wisely kept this to herself.

"And it's not just happening to me anymore," he added. "It's happening to you. You're on this list, and that makes you a part of this.

Maybe it is just a sick joke. But are you really willing to take that chance? Are you going to sleep well tonight, knowing that someone has collected all this information on us?"

Kate shifted uneasily.

"If you don't want to think this was set up by Craig, that's fine. But that means someone *else* is out there doing this." He lowered his voice. "Kate, it's okay to be scared. I'm a little freaked out myself. I think the reason you're fighting me so hard is because you're still trying to convince yourself this isn't happening. But deep down I think you do believe. And fighting all the time isn't going to solve anything. I need your help on this. I need you to be with me."

He stared at her, waiting for a response. She didn't care for his words one bit; the last part sounded rehearsed. It was his way of trying to draw her in, to get her to help him. It wasn't going to happen.

"All I need to know," she replied, "is if Craig took his own life. That's my only interest in any of this. And now if you don't mind, I'm pretty worn out and would like to go to sleep."

She expected him to argue and was surprised when he stood. "Okay. I'll see you in the morning."

"Hey," she said, thinking of it. "Could you do me a favor tomorrow?"

"What?" His voice was listless.

"I left my purse at Aunt Mary's. Can you get it for me? I don't think it'd be a good idea if I went over there. Not after what was said."

He questioned her with his eyes. Now he was going to ask what happened.

"Okay," he said mildly. "Sure."

"Andy?"

"Yeah?"

"Could you leave the basement light on for me?"

"Too bad Mr. Happy isn't here."

Kate smiled in spite of herself. She hadn't thought of her Mr. Happy night-light in years. It had guided her through many dark nights.

"Yeah," she agreed. "Definitely worth the two quarters Mom paid at that garage sale."

"Good night."

He retired up the stairs but only after turning on all the basement lights.

That suited Kate just fine.

TUESDAY

18

A dog was barking.

Andy came awake with a jerk and fell halfway off the couch. He scrambled to his feet and cursed when he saw it was past six. He had a dim memory of closing his eyes around four, but only to relax, not to sleep. There was a half-smoked cigarette between his fingers, and he guiltily tossed it in the ashtray.

He went to the kitchen and caught a drink from the faucet using his hands. His stomach tightened into a hard knot, and he did his best to ignore it. Hunger wasn't his primary concern. The first order of business was clean clothes and a visit to Mary's. Hopefully she would be more receptive this visit, especially regarding Craig's alleged brain tumor. If not, then it was onto the second order of business: revisiting the cans in the garage. Nothing out of the ordinary had been found during his initial search, but it still felt like too much of a coincidence to overlook. Plus, he was running out of ideas. His last theory—an aluminum recycling center on Fortieth Street—had been pretty thin to begin with, but he had still been disappointed when he learned there was no Fortieth Street. Not in Mortom, anyway. And he had to believe the clue referred to something in Mortom, or how else could he expect to find it? That was another reason why the aluminum cans in the garage were so tempting: every clue he had found so far had come from inside the house.

He passed by his duffel bag without a glance (the original plan had been to stay in Mortom one night, and he had packed for just that) and went into Craig's room. He stripped a blue T-shirt from a closet hanger and turned to the dresser for socks. His eyes immediately went to the open drawer—the drawer he *knew* had been shut when he had first been inside the room.

"Okay," he said, trying to rid his paranoia by speaking out loud. "If someone came into the house and was searching for something, why would they leave it open?"

The answer was simple: they wouldn't. If someone had been snooping, they would have left things the way they were found. That was the way it worked. End of story.

He found a pair of discolored socks and pulled them over his feet. Back in the kitchen he jotted a quick note: "Went to Mary's to get purse."

He slipped on his shoes and patted himself down to make sure he wasn't forgetting anything. The piece of tin was in his shirt pocket along with his cigarettes. For better or worse, he was ready to face the day.

He paused at the front door as he thought of Kate downstairs. She slept like the dead, and the last thing he wanted was to leave the house unlocked. Of course, no one had been in the house before, so there was no reason to be worried. And besides, this was Mortom, not Luther. People *could* leave their doors unlocked.

Still he lingered, his hand on the knob, his mind in a knot. It was such a simple thing, such a small choice to make . . . yet there he stood, wasting time, unable to decide.

"Hell," he said aloud.

He locked the door and shut it behind him. He was locking it because that was what people did when they left a house. It was perfectly normal. If he believed either of them were in any sort of danger, they would have left town long ago.

He hurried down the steps but only after shaking the knob to make sure the house was secure.

Just to be safe.

19

Kate stayed in bed a full five minutes after hearing the front door close, just to be certain Andy was gone and not coming back. She didn't have the energy to deal with him this early—not on the tiny fits of sleep she had managed to steal. It was his words from the night before that still infested her thoughts, or more importantly—his sincerity. Or lack of. He had no interest in the good of the family; he was doing it all for himself. Doing it for the game. She felt this so strongly she even found herself questioning the sheet of paper he had shown her with all their personal information. Deep down she couldn't believe Andy had planted it in a pathetic attempt to get her involved, but just having the thought made her wonder. Desperate people did desperate things. Her biggest problem now was deciding how desperate her brother had become.

Or how desperate he might get.

She wearily made her way up the staircase and winced at the lingering smell of rat. It was faint, but enough to make her stomach do a flip. For the first time she wondered if her nausea was something as simple as stress. Summers were made for relaxing and recharging, not dabbling in conspiracy theories.

The inside of the refrigerator was still empty (for some reason it hadn't magically filled itself with food during the night), but she found a can of frozen orange juice in the freezer. Five minutes to thaw and she would be set.

Her face twisted into a grimace as she saw the bowl inside the sink. It was the bowl Andy had used to sterilize the key, and she wasn't about to set her breakfast anywhere near it.

She grabbed the towel hanging from the stove and wrapped it around her hand. The bowl was heavy, even empty, and she barely had it out of the sink before it slipped from her grasp and shattered against the floor.

"Perfect," she mumbled.

Her eyes moved around the kitchen. She had seen a broom before; the trick was remembering where . . .

"Basement."

She was halfway down the staircase when she heard the screen door open. This was all she needed; Andy was already back, and she was going to run into him face to face.

She let out an irritated sigh and waited for the front door to open. Instead she heard a soft knock. She reached for it without thinking, then jumped when the knob rattled. The screen door shut and she heard footsteps trailing off.

She stared at the door, listening to her heart. It had to be Andy. He had locked the door when he left, had no key, and was trying to get back inside as quietly as possible in case she was still asleep. It was a perfectly logical explanation . . . except this was Andy. He *wasn't* polite or considerate. He was more likely to be leaning on the doorbell or banging the window.

The seconds passed. She told herself to open the door and look but couldn't bring herself to do it. What she *would* do was go into the living room and look out the front window. And if she didn't see the pickup in the driveway . . .

She cursed silently under her breath. This was Andy's fault; he was making her paranoid. Anyone could have been at the door. For all she knew it was Debbie, dropping off another kerosene casserole. People in small towns didn't lock their doors, and Debbie had probably been trying to set one inside the foyer.

She reached for the knob again, this time with more conviction, and froze when she heard heavy footsteps on the back deck. Something thumped the patio door, and she shrank toward the lower staircase. It almost sounded like a fist hitting glass—

There was another thump—louder this time—and she scrambled into the basement. She stood there, breathing heavily and feeling dumb. She was in a town where violence was so nonexistent they didn't have local police, and she was cowering in the basement because someone—probably her stupid brother—was trying to find a door that was unlocked so he could get back inside. Did she really think someone was trying to get her? They had only been in town for a little over two days; that was barely long enough to make friends, let alone enemies. Outside of Debbie and Aunt Mary, she hadn't spoken with or crossed paths with anyone else . . . Had she?

She tried to push the thought from her head. Whoever it was, they would go away. If she stayed quiet, everything would be fine and they would leave.

There was a sound from the garage and she whirled toward the connecting door. The doorknob was fitted with a simple turn lock—the same kind she had on her bathroom at home.

She stared at it, her mind drawing a blank, horror threatening to overtake her. Did *up* mean it was locked? It had to be. Andy had been in the garage last night, and if he had the hindsight to lock the front door when he left, surely he would have locked the door to the garage—

The doorknob began to slowly turn . . .

20

Andy gritted his teeth and knocked again. Mary had to be awake; all old people were up at the butt crack of dawn, and it was going on seven.

He surveyed the house, looking for signs of life. All the shades were drawn, including the ones on the second floor. Mary was either hiding, gone . . . or maybe in the backyard.

He followed his feet around the house. The backyard was filled with more junk, but no Mary. The whole day was ahead of him and he was stuck. Without Mary there was no information. And without information there was nothing to go on, just a handful of dead leaves and a piece of tin with the number forty.

He headed back to the truck, wondering if the station was open this early, or if he even had money to spend. Funds were running dangerously low, and part of him was afraid to open his wallet to check the damage. There was always Kate to hit up for cash . . .

"If she had her purse," he reminded himself.

His eyes swept the property, looking for a place to leave a note, and he nearly choked on his breath when he saw the mailbox.

Spray-painted across the side was the number forty.

He stared at it, afraid to blink. Two numbers, faded and weathered, barely worth a second glance.

It was the most beautiful sight he had ever seen.

He moved to the tree that shaded the house. The base was huge, and he did a slow examination of the ground, checking for loose dirt. The earth was unbroken; nothing had been buried there.

"Because the arrow points up," he said, lifting his head.

His eyes widened when he saw the birdhouse. It was halfway up the tree, dangling from a branch that was less than a foot away from the roof.

Without hesitation he grabbed the lowest branch. His feet scrambled against the base and found a small nub. With a grunt he managed to work himself up and almost immediately had to fight to catch his breath. In his youth he had scaled trees effortlessly. One summer he and some friends had constructed a tree house in their backyard, dragging up lumber while balancing on fingers and toes. That seemed like not only another time, but another life, too.

His hand wavered as it reached for the branch above his head. This was going to be the equivalent of a pull-up, something he also hadn't done since his youth.

His fingers curled around the branch, and he found himself stuck, unable to summon any more strength. His arm muscles were shaking. Five feet from the ground and he was already winded. What he needed was a ladder. A ladder would get him on the roof, and from there the birdhouse was an easy reach . . .

It was a pointless thought. There was no ladder, and it wasn't as if he could ask to borrow one from a neighbor. There was only one way he was getting up this tree.

He looked at the birdhouse for motivation. Something was written on the bottom in red paint. He squinted, trying to make it out. A bead of sweat dribbled into his eye and he wiped it away impatiently. The letters slowly came into focus: "CM."

Craig Moore.

His left foot slipped, and he fell forward with a cry, blindly grabbing the branch near his head with both hands. For a moment he was suspended, both feet dangling in the air. His feet found the branch below and he pulled himself into the base of the tree.

He stood there for an eternity, feeling like an idiot, afraid to move. Thirty years old and he was physically bankrupt. His mother had been right: beer and cigarettes had ruined him.

He drew in a breath, reached up, and locked his left hand around the branch the best he could. All he had to do was concentrate and focus. He was old, but not an old man. A little slower and heavier, but still capable. This was just a test of mental fortitude. It had nothing to do with strength.

His other hand shot out and grabbed the branch tightly. A small wind had picked up, carrying the stench of the dump with it. It was nothing compared to the rat. He blocked it out.

He slowly began pulling himself up, feet kicking wildly at the air. His breath locked as his arm muscles began to scream. With his last bit of strength he flung his right leg over the branch and let out a triumphant cry.

"Shit on me," he gasped.

He was there. He had done it.

He stood on rubber legs. The roof was no more than an arm's length away, and he grabbed on to the gutter with both hands for balance. The birdhouse was directly above his head, no more than a reach. All he had to do was free up one hand and grab it. Easy as pie.

He commanded his hand to reach up and take the prize. But his hand seemed to have other ideas about where it wanted to be and tightened its grip on the gutter.

His eyes moved to the ground. A fall at this height wouldn't kill him, but it would hurt like hell. Heights had never bothered him before . . . not until this moment, anyway. At this moment they bothered him quite a bit.

The wind picked up again, tickling the nape of his neck. He screamed at himself to move. It wasn't just about being discovered anymore; his legs were trembling, and if he waited much longer, he wouldn't have the strength to climb down.

"Okay," he huffed. "Okay, okay, okay."

He unlatched his right hand and wrapped his fingers around the birdhouse. It came free, and he tossed it on the roof before grabbing the gutter again for balance.

"I got you," he whispered . . . but the words fell flat as he stared at his accomplishment. The birdhouse was made out of wood, not metal, and the hole was about the size of a quarter. Not much of an opening to hide something inside.

He picked it up and shook it, momentarily forgetting his fear. There was no sound. All at once he felt an insane urge to break it open right there, but that was stupid, especially if something small was inside. A sheet of paper wouldn't make a sound, and he couldn't risk losing it to a gust of wind. He needed to carry it to the ground and examine it. Something had to be inside—everything pointed to this.

Still he lingered, not liking it. He had found the number forty, had followed the arrow to the leaves . . . and still it didn't feel right. But it *had* to be right. What else was there?

He readjusted his grip, knocking away leaves from the gutter. They were everywhere. They were especially bad where he was standing, almost as if—

His breath stopped.

Directly in front of him, no more than a foot from his face, was a small cloth sack.

Wedged into the *aluminum* gutter . . .

21

"I feel like such an idiot," Kate said, wiping her cheeks. She shifted on the couch and grabbed another tissue. "I've been so emotional lately . . . I don't know what's wrong with me. I'm sorry."

Mary waved away the apology. "No, I'm the one who's sorry, coming over here and scaring you half out of your wits. When I saw the pickup was gone, I figured you two were out at breakfast, and I'd just leave your purse inside the house. I shouldn't have done it. It's not my place to be here. It's Andrew's now."

"No," Kate sniffed, "it's fine. I was going to come over and get the purse, but after last night . . ."

She trailed off, unsure how to finish. The last thing she wanted was to upset Mary by rehashing their conversation.

"It's okay," Mary said. "I shouldn't have been so sharp with you. When you asked me if I ever thought . . . if I thought that Craig . . ."

Kate realized she was holding her breath and quickly pushed it out. "I never meant to imply—"

"Course you didn't," Mary said with a smile. Tears glistened in her eyes. "It was just hard hearing it spoken aloud, I suppose."

Kate forced a nod. "And I only said it because I thought you were leading into it. It hadn't even crossed my mind until it slipped out."

The lie easily passed her lips, and Kate didn't care for the feeling one bit. Andy was rubbing off on her.

"I haven't been here in a while," Mary said, rising from the couch. She lifted a book from the coffee table. "Craig never was one for cleaning. I always offered to do it for him, but he never let me. I figured it was the least I could do, seeing how he always came over and took care of the man stuff at my place."

Mary slid the book into the bookcase. Her eyes drifted around the living room. Kate watched without speaking, unsure what to say.

"I gave him this last Christmas," Mary said, pointing to the picture above the television. It was a print of a wooden cabin surrounded by trees and snow. Mary straightened it with a small smile. "This was where Craig always yearned to be . . . off somewhere by himself, trapped with his games and puzzles. Sometimes I thought it was his only passion in life."

Mary stared at the picture almost lovingly.

"Could you ask Andrew if I might have this?" Mary asked. "I can look at it and pretend it's a picture of Craig living in a cabin far away. Like a picture he sent me in the mail. I can pretend he's inside, propped up in a chair, maybe reading a book."

Kate stood. "Of course you can have it."

"No," Mary said, shaking her head. "Only if Andrew says it's okay. It's his now, and we have to respect that."

"Aunt Mary, how did Craig . . . *feel* about Andy?"

For a moment Mary said nothing. Kate wasn't entirely sure why she had asked the question; it had just come out.

"When Craig was growing up," Mary answered quietly, "I always used Andrew as an example. A boy needs someone to look up to. Usually it's someone older, not younger, but in many ways that worked to my advantage."

"Advantage?"

"When Craig was five, he was still sucking his thumb. So I would say, 'Andrew doesn't suck his thumb and he's only two.' Course, Andrew *never* sucked his thumb, but I didn't mention that. And sure as rain, Craig stopped sucking his thumb. I used Andrew as a role model for everything. For the most part it worked, but as Craig grew older I think he began to struggle with it. He would always rise to the challenge, but at the same time he took offense, like I was more proud of my sister's son than I was my own son. I think he began to feel like he had something to prove. Maybe I was too hard on the boy, but it wasn't easy being a single parent. Lord knows I did my best. I even almost got married once, not out of love, but just to get him a daddy . . ."

Kate found herself leaning forward, waiting for more. No one in the family ever spoke of Craig's father, especially Mary.

"But what about you?" Mary asked.

Kate blinked. "Me?"

"I can't believe no man has swept you away yet. Tell this old aunt of yours why you're not married. You're not one of those lesbians, are you?"

Kate gave a surprised laugh. "No, not at all. There have been boyfriends, just no husband material. I was seeing a pretty decent guy for a while, but things got complicated. It's different in a big city. Most people put work ahead of family. Family seems not to mean as much there."

"Family is important," said Mary. "Above all else."

Kate waited for more, but Mary only smiled. "I best be on my way. My legs get cranky if I stand too long."

"I'll ask Andy about that picture. And if there's anything else you can think of—"

"I don't suppose there will be. I have all my photographs of Craig growing up, and I can always look at those. You just make sure to come see me again before you leave. I do enjoy speaking with you."

Kate noticed that Andy wasn't included in the invitation. "I'll walk you out."

"No need. I've done it a hundred times before, and I can do it one last time. Has Andrew spoken about what he'll do with the house? I don't imagine he'll want to keep it."

"The bank manager will be auctioning it off."

"Mr. Thatcher will do just fine," Mary said with a nod. "He's a good man."

Kate followed her down the staircase anyway, feeling something more needed to be said, but not wanting to risk saying the wrong thing. From this moment on, Craig's death was taboo, and she wasn't going to bring it up again, no matter what.

"Yes," Mary said softly.

"Hmm?" Kate asked.

Mary was facing the door with one hand on the knob. Kate gently touched her shoulder.

"Craig," Mary said in a hollow voice. She turned her head but didn't meet Kate's eyes. "Yes . . . I think he may have ended his life."

A lump rose in Kate's throat. "Mary, we don't know that. You said yourself—"

"I told him."

"Told him what?"

"I never once said anything about the man, but after Craig found out about the tumor . . . he kept asking me and asking me, and finally I told him . . . and I will never forgive myself for that."

And without another word, Mary was gone out the door.

22

Andy's chest loosened as he pulled into the gas station and saw the "Open" sign in the window. It was one hurdle down, anyway. Talking to Nate was probably a long shot, but it was hopefully a start in the right direction.

He killed the ignition and took a moment to plan his approach. *Hey, Nate, I found these stuffed in the gutter of Mary's house. Any ideas what they might open?*

"Subtle as a hurricane," he mumbled.

He took the key ring from his shirt pocket. Three keys. The first was long with a clover-shaped head and looked straight out of an antique shop. The next key was much smaller, had an oval head, and didn't look nearly as old or worn. The last key was silver and shiny—a padlock key, for sure. Attached to the key ring was a small plastic skeleton. It was a cheap little trinket—something that might be found in a vending machine for kids—and one of the emerald eyes had either fallen out or been removed. Whatever the case, it was worth noting. He was still pissed at himself for believing the key (not the rat) was the actual clue, and he wasn't about to trivialize anything at this point.

Regardless, the big key was the place to start, and hopefully Nate could get him moving in the right direction. Or any direction for that matter.

The door to the station was propped open with a brick, and he found Nate sprawled in a recliner, drinking a bottle of soda.

"I was wondering when I was going to see you again," Nate said with a grin.

"You open for business?"

"Oh yeah." He tried to heave himself up from the chair and didn't quite make it. "We just don't see too many people this early."

"You don't have to get up—"

"Good exercise," Nate wheezed. He managed to get to his feet and let out a chuckle. "Down and up, up and down. Story of my life. What can I do you for?"

"I was wondering if you had any ideas about these keys," Andy said, holding up the ring and watching closely for any flicker of recognition. "It's the old key I'm most curious about."

"Hoping to find some hidden treasure?" Nate asked with a crooked grin. There was amusement in his voice but nothing else.

Andy smiled. "You never know."

"Charlie Sumac at the hardware store might have some thoughts. He's been there about fifty years and knows a lot about everything. I'd be tempted to stop in and pay him a visit."

"Is he there now?"

"Hey!" Nate shouted. "You're not welcome here!"

Andy took a startled step back, momentarily confused. When he realized Nate was looking past him, he turned and saw the problem firsthand.

The kid standing in the doorway was almost textbook white trash: sleeveless flannel shirt, jeans torn and stained, one boot wrapped in duct tape. Greasy black hair poked out from the baseball cap parked backward on his head. His grin was wide but uninviting, as if he were enjoying a joke known only to him.

Nate said, "I told you before not to come around—"

"Blah, blah, *yeah* . . . I hear ya." The kid scratched at the anthill of stubble on his chin. "Need some supplies is all. Shippin out of town in a few days and figured you'd be all sad if I didn't stop by one last time. You know . . . sort of like a farewell shopping trip and all."

The kid tossed Andy a wink. Nate crossed his arms and said nothing.

"Cigarettes and beer?" The kid's eyes jumped between the two of them. "Come on now; can't expect a fella to function without the basics of life."

"Harlan," said Nate, "I'm gonna count to three—"

"Okay," the kid said with an innocent shrug. "No sweat off my balls. I'll go to the competition. But maybe I'll see ya again."

This last comment was not directed toward Nate. Andy didn't drop his eyes until the kid was out the door.

"Harlan Shawler," Nate said with a grunt. "My nephew, I'm sorry to say. Lives over in Keota. Hitchhikes over here to cause trouble. Believe it or not, he was friends with Craig."

"Really? *That* guy?"

"Remember how I told you Craig drove to Keota every Saturday night? It was for a weekly poker game. Craig mentioned it one night after filling up. Said Harlan showed up from time to time. Funny thing, thinking about those two in the same room together. Or Craig playing cards, for that matter."

Andy nodded thoughtfully.

"Anyhow," Nate smiled, quickly returning to his jovial self. "Must be my lucky year. I never figured Harlan to leave these parts, but I guess I got something to look forward to now."

"Hey," Andy said, thinking of it, "does anything special happen around here on Friday the thirteenth?"

"I close early on Friday's."

"No, I mean with the town. Anniversary or anything? Celebration of any kind?"

Nate laughed. "Sometimes the kids get drunk and stupid, but that's about every Friday around here."

"Gotcha. You think your friend Charlie is there now?"

Nate checked his watch. "He usually opens the place around eight. His son works the afternoon shift, so I'd get over there before noon if you want to catch him."

"On my way. I'm just gonna grab a couple of things and then I'll be out of your hair."

"Buy the whole store. Then I can retire."

Andy laughed and started toward the cooler. He tossed a casual glance out the door and saw the kid leaning through the driver-side window of his truck.

"Hey!" Andy shouted.

The kid took off down the street without looking back.

"What happened?" Nate asked, coming up behind him.

"He was in my truck."

"Harlan!" Nate yelled. "You get your ass back here!"

"No, it's okay. Let him go."

"No-good punk," Nate grumbled. "You let me know if anything's missing, and I'll get my brother on the horn and get it back."

Andy gave an absent nod. "He was probably just looking for cigarettes or something. It's fine."

He watched until the kid passed from view, unaware his hand had closed so tightly around the key ring that his knuckles had drained white.

23

Kate was out the front door and down the steps the second Andy pulled into the driveway. "Where have you been?"

Her patience slipped as he climbed out without as much as an upward glance. Something was in his hand and she forced herself not to look. Whatever it was, she didn't want to know.

"Andy!"

"Yeah?" He lifted his head. "What's up?"

Kate struggled to keep her voice steady. "I asked where you've been."

"Mary's house," he said vaguely. "Then over to the gas station and down to the hardware store. There was a sign on the door that said he was home with his ailing dog. Can you believe that?"

"Aunt Mary was here," Kate said. "She showed up shortly after you left."

"Yeah, I didn't get your purse. But I found what I was looking for in the gutter."

"Gutter? What are you talking about?"

"The *leaves*. They led me to Mary's roof. I found this."

Kate gave the ring a brief glance. "Whatever. Listen, Mary said something strange right before she left. Something along the lines of, 'I shouldn't have told him, but he asked.' I think she was talking about Craig's father."

"Oh yeah?" Andy turned the key ring over in his hands as he studied it. "Father, huh?"

"Yes," Kate said irritably. He wasn't listening or hearing her. "*Craig's* father. Maybe he is a part of this after all. Maybe you were right."

"Maybe," said Andy, "it's to an old building somewhere around here."

"What is?"

"This old key—"

"Can you listen to me for one second of your life? It's no wonder Carol left you! You can't focus on anything but your own selfish needs!"

She had his full attention now. Whether or not she still wanted it was another question.

"You just can't leave it alone, can you?" His voice was like a shard of glass. "You want to know about my *selfish* needs? Fine, let me spell it out for you. Carol got pregnant and she wasn't sure it was mine."

"What?"

"Come on, Kate. We've all heard the story a hundred times. Husband works long hours at the office, wife feels unloved and seeks attention elsewhere."

"Andy," Kate said, cupping a hand over her mouth. "I had no idea—"

"That stuff like this happens in real life? It's the sort of thing that only happens in books and movies, right?" A bitter laugh escaped his mouth. "Do you know what I did after she told me? Do you want to know what your selfish, uncaring brother told his wife of seven years after hearing this?"

Kate tried to speak but only a croak came out.

"I told her I still loved her," he said roughly. "I said I would stand by her side, regardless of what happened or what we found out. The next day she took some things and left. She wouldn't say where she was going. She said she was too ashamed to face me and needed time alone. I didn't want her to go, but I let her. And then I fell apart. I couldn't eat or sleep. I couldn't focus on anything. I didn't quit my job, Kate. I got fired for not showing up."

"Andy . . ."

"I heard from her a week later." There was no emotion on his face now. "She said she lost the baby. I asked if she had a miscarriage. All she would say was the baby was gone, and it was for the best."

Kate stared at him, horrified. Andy's eyes narrowed into slits, warning her not to ask the question that was on the tip of her tongue.

"And that was that," he finished. "She wouldn't say anything more about it, no matter how much I asked. A few days later she contacted a divorce lawyer, and that was that."

"Why?" Kate asked on the verge of tears. "Why didn't you just tell us?"

"Because it's nobody's business!" he shouted. "It doesn't concern you, and it doesn't concern Mom or Dad! It's nobody's business but my own!"

"Is everything okay?" asked a timid voice.

Kate turned with a start. Debbie was at the edge of the sidewalk, staring uneasily at Andy.

"Yeah," Kate smiled, wiping her eyes. "Yeah, hon . . . We were just talking. This is my brother, Andy."

Andy grabbed the grocery bag from the bed of the truck. "I'll be inside."

"Where did you get those?" Debbie asked.

"Gas station," he said, starting up the driveway. "Cheap deals and great prices for all."

"I meant Craig's keys to the old cemetery."

Andy spun so quickly he almost lost the bag from his hands. "What did you say?"

Debbie tossed an uncertain glance at Kate. "I . . . I just wondered where you found Craig's keys."

For a moment Andy seemed incapable of speech. His mouth hung open. He set the bag on the ground and held out the key ring.

"These go to the *old* cemetery?" he asked in a voice that wasn't quite steady. "Are you sure? How would you know something like that?"

"I gave him the skeleton." Debbie's eyes jumped back and forth between Andy and Kate. "I thought it was funny, because . . . you know, he worked in a cemetery."

Andy shook the big key into his hand. "Do you know what this one opens?"

"The outside gate. It doesn't close or lock anymore, but that's what it's for."

"And these?" Andy demanded, making her flinch. "What about these two small keys?"

Debbie looked to Kate. Kate met her eyes but said nothing. Andy was scaring the hell out of this poor girl and she was doing nothing to stop him. At that moment she hated herself as well as Andy.

"The work shed," said Debbie. "Craig said he lost them when Grandpa asked for them back."

"Grandpa?"

Kate moved between them. "Andy, that's enough."

"All I'm doing is asking—"

"*Debbie!*"

This new voice came from across the street, and it took Kate no more than a moment to identify the man racing up the sidewalk.

"Debbie!" Ricky shouted again, leveling a finger at her. "Get inside the house!"

Andy glowered at Kate. "Guess you neglected to mention you met Debbie, huh?"

Debbie fled across the street. Andy started to follow and Kate grabbed his arm. "Andy, *don't*."

"Don't *what*?" he said, shaking off her grip. "I just want to ask him—"

The front door to Ricky's house shut loudly enough to turn both their heads.

"Thanks, Kate. Thanks a bunch."

"Look, I'm sorry about what I said, and I'm sorry about how I said it. But you have to get yourself under control. I'm not going to stand idly by and watch you harass children and old men."

"Worry about yourself, okay? I'm a big boy. I can play with whoever I want."

"Please don't get involved with Debbie's grandfather. He's not someone . . ." She stopped herself, trying to choose her words carefully. "He worked with Craig, okay? But that doesn't necessarily mean anything, even if there was some sort of falling out between the two of them."

His eyes flicked up, and she realized she had just given him information he had not possessed.

"I'm going for a walk," he said flatly. "My keys are in the truck. Feel free to *not* be here when I return."

He knocked over the bag of groceries with his foot as he passed. Kate slowly bent down and began shoving the items back inside the bag, not allowing herself to look over her shoulder . . . no matter how much she could feel a pair of cold eyes on her from across the street.

24

Andy stood at the entrance of the old cemetery with one hand resting on the wrought-iron fence. One thing was certain: this place wasn't going to be friendly after dark.

Headstones were packed tightly at every turn, and the ground was uneven and cluttered with dead tree branches. Countless places to trip and fall, especially if the moon decided to hide behind a patch of cloud.

He straightened up as a car sped past, listening to the motor until it faded into background noise. Standing there getting spooked was the last thing he needed to worry about—that would be accomplished easily enough when he returned later that night. Right now was for checking things out.

His eyes moved to the work shed. Even from twenty yards he could easily discern the shiny padlock hanging from the oversized door. Technically it was breaking and entering, but what choice did he have? Groundskeeper Ricky Simms wasn't about to give him permission to enter, especially now.

Some sort of falling out, Kate had said.

All this time he had been convinced Craig's death had been a suicide . . . but what if it had actually been a homicide? Ricky pushes Craig off the cliff, makes it look like an accident, then sets up the game for some sort of crazed revenge.

He studied on this a moment longer before shaking his head. There was too much evidence pointing to Craig: everything from the handwriting of the letters to the fact that all the clues (so far) had been found at Craig's or Mary's house. If Ricky was involved, it was in some other way.

"What are you doing here?"

Andy spun around and found himself face to face with Ricky Simms. He hadn't even heard him come up behind him.

"You don't belong here," said Ricky.

Andy forced himself not to swallow. "I came to pay my respects to Craig."

"He's in the other graveyard."

"My mistake."

They stared at one other. Ricky had to be in his sixties, but he was built thick and hard—the type of man who had never sat behind a desk in his life. He also overshadowed Andy by at least three inches and had a neck the size of a tree stump.

"Andy Crowl," Andy said, offering his hand. "Craig's cousin. My aunt said you two worked together?"

"I treated that boy like a son. Gave him a job and invited him over for dinners in my home. And he stabbed me in the back."

"Sorry to hear—"

"Just cut the crap. I don't know what you're up to, but I've been watching you. Going all over town, asking questions, acting like you have every right to be here. Believe me, you don't."

Andy felt a catch in his throat. "Whatever happened between you and Craig has nothing to do with me."

"He was your cousin. You share the same blood."

"Ah," Andy said, trying to keep his tone light. "Guilt by association, is that what this is about? Craig and I didn't even know each other very well."

"He left everything to you over his own mother. Seems pretty friendly to me."

Andy opened his mouth but nothing came out.

"Just stay out of my way," Ricky said. "And tell your wife to stay away from my granddaughter. If you're not man enough to do it, someone else will do it for you."

"Kate's my sister," Andy replied, trying to control the anger in his voice. Light perspiration had broken on his face and arms. "I'm not married."

"I suppose a man like you wouldn't be. God help your children if you ever have any."

Andy felt all the blood rush to his face. "What does that mean?"

"You've been warned," Ricky said, turning away.

"Hey, I asked you a question—"

He wheeled around and poked Andy hard enough to drive him back a step. "You do *not* want to mess with me." He gave him a final, measured stare before moving off without so much as a backward glance.

"What is it you think I did?" Andy shouted after him.

Ricky disappeared into a clump of trees, and Andy set off down the road in a huff. He had better things to do than waste time here. Whatever had happened between Ricky and Craig had nothing to do with him.

"Bunch of shit," he said over his shoulder. The cemetery was already out of sight behind the curve. "I didn't do anything."

His hand went to his chest. There was going to be a bruise there and a decent-sized one, at that. It was the first time in his life he had been assaulted by anyone, let alone someone old enough to be his father. Didn't that prove Ricky was capable of violence? Was it really that far-fetched to think he could have thrown Craig off a cliff in a fit of rage?

"No." He spoke the words aloud, but quietly. "Not far-fetched at all."

He stole another glance behind him, wishing he had his truck. He was stuck in the middle of nowhere with a possible lunatic, thanks to Kate. Not only was she intent on invading his personal life; she was also going to get him killed.

Something touched his shoulder, and he spun around, both hands jumping protectively to his face. There was only the wind, shaking the trees and blowing errant leaves across the road.

"Just ghosts," he said, running a cupped hand across his mouth. His brow narrowed as he caught sight of the white glob on his sleeve. It almost looked like toothpaste . . .

"Son of a bitch," he hissed.

It was poop. *Bird* poop. He had been walking down the road, minding his own business, and a goddamn bird had just pooped on his shoulder.

"For the love of God," he muttered, stripping a leaf from a low branch. The glob was already halfway down his arm, and he managed to get more on his fingers than the leaf as he wiped.

"Are you kidding me?" he shouted.

His hand froze midair as Ricky's truck crept around the curve and shuddered to a stop. The grill grinned at him with tiny cavities of rust. Ricky sat motionless inside.

"Go around," Andy said under his breath.

Ricky dogged the gas pedal, taunting him.

"*Go,*" he said, raising his voice. His heart accelerated from a fast run into a gallop. "You've got plenty of room."

The engine revved. Andy forced himself to stand his ground. It wouldn't matter if he moved an inch or a mile; this had nothing to do with the road. Ricky was a bully—plain and simple—and it was going to end here and now.

"I'm not budging," he said loudly. "I can—"

It was all he got out before the truck lurched forward on squealing tires.

25

Kate wasn't entirely surprised when she ended up in Keota (the urge to get out of Mortom had been almost overwhelming, and Keota was the closest town she knew), but it was pure serendipity that she happened upon the courthouse. One minute she was looking for a café to rest her bones; the next minute she was driving past the building that held all the birth and death records for Van Duten County. Coincidence or not, the opportunity was too tempting to pass up.

The registrar's office was directly inside the front door, and her heart picked up speed as she approached the counter. It was guilt she was feeling—guilt at poking her nose where it shouldn't be. The same way she felt when a police cruiser pulled onto the street behind her, even when she was doing nothing wrong. Innate guilt was something that had haunted her most of her adult life, a fun side effect of her Catholic upbringing. Amen.

The woman behind the counter was twirling a strand of autumn-red hair between two fingers and leafing through a magazine. The jaded expression on her face seemed to say, *I'm way too good to be working here, but you know how it is.*

"Hello," Kate said with a smile. "I was interested in looking up a record—"

"Go through the second door and help yourself," the woman answered without glancing up. "It's all self-serve."

Kate smiled again, this time with more effort. "Thank you."

She followed the counter to the end and stepped through the open door. Hundreds of books stared back at her from wooden bookcases. All were cased in white, plastic covers and dated along the spine. A bank of computers sat to her right, but all the screens were black. Above each terminal was a small sign that read, "Index Search."

"Is it safe to assume you need some direction?"

The voice was female and friendly and belonged to a middle-aged woman with thick glasses and rosy cheeks. A pink pencil poked out from behind her ear, and for some reason Kate found that reassuring.

"I'm looking for birth records. The woman at the counter told me to come in, but I have no idea what to do."

"Yeah, I heard you talking to Lynette over there. Don't pay her any mind. The only time she's helpful is when men come in. Then it's all boobs and giggles."

Kate fought back a grin.

"I'm the deputy, Faye. Only three of us here in the office. Myself, the recorder, and you already met Ms. Part-part-time."

Kate had to ask. "Part-*part*-time?"

Faye dropped her voice. "Lynette works here part-time, but only works *part* of the time she's here. Mostly she can be found painting her nails at her desk or reading magazines. She's a real treat."

"I'll try not to bother her too much," Kate replied somberly.

Faye chuckled and motioned at the far wall. "The oversized books underneath the counter are the births. They're a bit of a chore to lift but pretty straightforward to maneuver. The indexes are in the front of each book and in alphabetical order. Find the last name, and that will tell you what page the record is on. Holler if you get stuck."

"I will. Thanks again."

The birth books were shelved horizontally and numbered by year. Kate calculated the math in her head as she squatted in front of them. Craig was (had been) thirty-three, three years older than Andy.

"Nineteen seventy-four," she said.

She latched on to the second book from the bottom and wrestled it onto the counter with a grunt. "Oversized" was an understatement: the book was a foot and a half in length and at least five inches thick.

The spine crackled as she opened the cover, and she carefully flipped through the index until she came to the letter *M*. Her eyes followed her finger as she scanned through the listings.

"Moore . . ."

She found it halfway down the first page: Moore, Craig. Page 287.

Her pulse quickened as she thumbed through the pages. She told herself again she wasn't doing anything wrong; lots of people researched genealogy. Lots of people were interested in family history, as was she.

Craig Moore was the third record on the page, and she quickly found the box she was after: "Father's Name."

"David Ward," she read aloud.

She lifted her head, trying to decide if that sounded correct. She knew so little about the man. Mary had met him in college, there had been a whirlwind romance that ended in pregnancy, and shortly thereafter he had died in a car accident. Outside of that, Kate knew nothing.

The death records were on the next shelf over. She found the book of the same year and lifted it to the counter. If David Ward had died while Mary was pregnant, his death record would be inside. It was almost too easy.

Kate ran her finger down the *W*'s and found nothing. The next page had one Ward, but the first name was Brian. The page after that went into the *X*'s. She double-checked the date on the spine: 1974–1975. She was in the right book . . .

She found Faye at her desk and served up an apologetic smile. "Can I bother you again?"

"Bother away."

"Where does the death certificate get recorded when someone dies?"

"In the county where the death occurred. But if the person dies while out of town, a county resident copy is recorded in the county of their permanent residence."

"Thank you," she said, feeling like a fool. Craig's birth record was there because he had been born in Keota, but Mary had met the father in Luther. What she needed to do was check the courthouse there. Of course, if she looked and found nothing, it would only prove the man hadn't lived or died in Luther. And if that was the case, the records could be anywhere in the state. Kate wanted to know if the man was alive or dead, and without coming right out and asking Mary, there would be no way to know.

She reshelved the death-record book, but lingered over the birth book, unsettled. She was positive she had heard the father's name at least once, and David Ward didn't sound right. But there it was, right in front of her face . . .

Her brow creased when she saw December 11 listed under "Date of Birth." Craig's birthday was in September; she was sure of it. Almost every Labor Day weekend of her youth had been marred by his "surprise" birthday visit, and more than once it had thrown wrenches into long weekend plans. It had to be a typo.

She quickly scanned through the record, her eyes jumping from box to box. County of residence . . . state of birth . . . mother's name . . .

"*Helen* Moore?"

She leaned forward, as if lessening the distance might change what was on the page. Again, plain as day: Helen Moore. It had to be a mistake, another typo. Unless . . .

She flipped back to the index and quickly scanned down the *M*'s again. Moore was a fairly common name, and it wasn't completely absurd to think there might be more than *one* Craig Moore in the book. That was more realistic than the record having multiple errors, anyway.

There were no other Craigs listed. She returned the book to its original spot and peered around the corner, looking for Faye. She was nowhere in sight. Against her better judgment, Kate approached Lynette, who was making a sign on colored paper: "Office Closed Tommorrow."

"Can I ask you a question?"

Lynette looked up with a wry smile: *Do I have a choice?*

"I was looking for a birth record and can't find it."

"Was he adopted? If he was adopted, the record at the county gets sealed."

"No. The parents were never married and the father died before he was born—"

"Single-parent births go directly to the state vital-records office," she said tonelessly. "You would have to write them and request it by mail."

"And they'd send me a copy?" Kate asked, mostly out of curiosity.

Gruffly: "Are you a family member?"

"Cousin."

"Only immediate family has entitlement. Parents, siblings, children, or grandparents. No aunt or uncles, no in-laws, no cousins."

"Thanks for all the information," Kate said with a pert smile. And then, unable to resist herself, she added, "And incidentally, *tomorrow* only has one *M*."

She hurried away without looking back, afraid of what obscene finger gesture might be following her out the door. Not that it mattered; she wouldn't be going back there again. Real life wasn't like the movies; a person couldn't just walk into a place and stumble across a vital piece of information. The only thing she knew for certain was that Aunt Mary hadn't been married when Craig was born, but she had known that already. She still didn't know anything more about his father.

"Let sleeping dogs lie," she said absently. It was one of her mother's favorite expressions, and it fit the situation perfectly. And why not? It was good advice, *sound* advice . . . and she told herself this over and over as she made her way across the street toward the coffee shop in search of a phone.

26

"Two visits in one day?" Nate asked with a grin. "With this much business, I could close early . . ."

His words tapered off as Andy dropped into the recliner and stared vacantly at the floor. Nate came from behind the counter and sat across from him.

"What can you tell me about Ricky Simms?" Andy asked.

Nate's brow immediately narrowed. "Why?"

"I just avoided becoming his new hood ornament by about six inches. It's painfully obvious the man doesn't care for me. I know it has something to do with Craig, but that's all I know." He leaned forward. "What *don't* I know?"

For a long time Nate didn't speak; Andy could almost see the gears moving inside his head.

"I pride myself on tending to my own business," Nate began, "and sometimes that's hard to do in a small town, especially with a place like this. Thirty years I've been on this job. Started part-time in high school. Mr. Kitz, the owner, took me on full-time after I did my part for the war effort. Even back then it was pretty much a one-man operation, and I think he mostly had me around for company. Like me, he never married, and running this place was what got him out of bed in the mornings. Until he broke his back and ended up in the hospital, that is to say. They told him he would never walk again, let alone stand. I showed up every day, unlocked the place, and worked it open to close. I visited him once a week, and every time I saw him he seemed to be worse. Physically he had healed the best he could, but his will to live had gone. There was nothing to keep him going. And when he died, everybody in town expected me to buy this place and run it, and that's what I did. I love the old dive, because it's the only thing I have in my life. It's what gets *me* out of bed in the mornings."

Andy fought to keep his voice steady. "No offense, Nate, but I don't really see—"

"All Ricky has is his granddaughter, Debbie. After his wife died, Debbie started coming down for the summers. There was no question it was a turning point for him. He was still foul most of the time, but his affection for her was obvious. That girl is the only joy Ricky has in his life, and he would do anything to protect her."

"Protect her from what? Craig? Because I'm seriously starting to wonder if Ricky had something to do with Craig's death."

"Bite your tongue," Nate said, but without conviction. His brow softened. "Andy, you have to understand this is a small town. You can't go around saying things like that, even to me. Word travels, whether a person wants it to or not."

"Look," Andy said, rising from the chair, "if you don't want to tell what you know, fine. I'm sure if I ask enough other people, eventually I'll find someone who will."

"Now just wait," Nate said, holding up one hand. "Don't be going away all irate. Just give me a minute."

Andy lingered a moment before dropping back into the chair. Nate pushed out a heavy sigh.

"If I speak of this, it stays in this room."

Andy nodded. "Of course."

"I would guess there are others who know about it, but only a few. You have to swear to me you won't repeat—"

"Nate, you said that already."

"It's about Debbie," Nate said quietly. "Something happened, and it's not good.

"Listen . . ."

27

Kate balanced the phone against her ear as she set her calling card on the table beside her untouched coffee. The smell alone was enough to make her stomach churn (coffee had never been her beverage of choice), but wrapping fingers around a warm mug was a pleasure all its own. Her bones seemed to be set on permanent chill—another fun new twist to the nausea and aches. It was especially bad around her chest, and she wondered if it wasn't some sort of flu. Only she could catch flu in the summer.

"Hello?"

Kate lifted the receiver to her mouth. "Mom, it's me."

"I was wondering when you were going to call. When did you two get home?"

"Actually, we're still in Mortom."

"You're still there?" There was a hint of alarm in her mother's voice. "I figured you two would have left yesterday. Didn't Andy get everything taken care of?"

"Well, some other stuff came up."

"Other stuff?"

Kate paused, unsure how to continue. She and her mother had always been close, but all at once she found herself uneasy. This wasn't run-of-the-mill conversation like money worries or dating woes; this was serious business that affected the immediate family. Once things like dead rats and brain tumors were thrown onto the table, there was no turning back.

"Kate?"

She took a deep breath. "Mom, what can you tell me about Craig's father?"

There was immediate silence.

"Mom? You there?"

"Why are you asking me this?" The light concern in her voice was gone, replaced by a tone that wasn't exactly anger, but close.

"I just . . . I've spoken with Aunt Mary a few times, and there's some stuff . . ."

Kate trailed off, trying to find the words. All at once she was five years old again, caught with both hands in the cookie jar.

"I just was wondering about Craig's father," she finished lamely.

More silence. Kate felt a small jolt of impatience as she waited for her mother to speak. She had expected some apprehension but not a full-blown shutout. All she wanted was some basic information.

"Leave it alone," her mother said sharply. "The man died and that's all there is to it. The poor woman has been through so much in her life . . . I don't know what she said or what you thought you heard, but leave it alone."

Kate was surprised to find some anger of her own. "I was just curious about the father. Is that so wrong?"

Kate waited for a response; none came.

"Mom?"

There was a series of clicks. She pressed the handset tighter against her ear and let out a startled cry when it began to beep.

"Great," she muttered, grabbing back the calling card.

She dialed again and found the line busy. Her mother was undoubtedly still holding the phone, unaware they had been disconnected.

"Everything okay, hon'?"

Kate smiled at the waitress. "Yeah, thanks. Phone problems."

"Wouldn't surprise me. That thing barely gets used anymore. Everybody has those cell phones nowadays."

"I suppose. I'm probably one of the few people in the world who doesn't own one yet."

The waitress laughed. "You and me both."

Kate reset the line with her finger and dialed again. Still busy. She hung up and told herself to let it go. She wasn't looking for an argument, and the only damage, at this point, was a tense phone call. Calling again would only make things worse, and it was obvious her mother had no intention of sharing what she knew.

Or what she was hiding.

"Stop," Kate whispered.

She was starting to sound like Andy, and that was the last thing anyone needed. It was over; she was done.

She left the café, wishing she had somewhere else to go but knowing there was only Mortom.

28

It was almost six when Kate pulled into the driveway, and any hope of Andy being gone was erased when she saw the front door standing open. They were going to have words, whether she wanted to or not.

She found him on the deck with a twelve-pack at his feet. He finished the can he was holding and set it on the railing.

"What can you tell me about Debbie?" he asked.

"Why?"

"Kate, please. No bullshit, no games. Just tell me."

She crossed her arms and met his eyes, trying to gauge his purpose. There was something there she couldn't quite discern—it almost looked like grief.

"She stays with her grandpa over the summers," Kate said, weighing each word carefully. "She was obviously fond of Craig. I get the impression she spent a lot of time over here. At least, she did before something happened between Craig and her grandpa."

"And what do you know about him? The grandfather?"

Again she hesitated. It was on the edge of her tongue to tell him what she had seen at the cemetery, but she couldn't bring herself to do it. She wasn't ready to open that door. Not yet.

"Not much," she said, knowing from the look in his eyes she had hesitated too long. "Why are you so interested?"

He dug a fresh can from the twelve-pack. "Care to join me?"

"No."

"A gift from Nate," he said with a bitter smile. "Giver of brew and teller of tales. Told me a tale about Debbie, in fact. Debbie and Ricky and our cousin, Craig. You're right about one thing: Debbie and Craig were fond of each other. So fond, in fact, that Craig took it upon himself . . ."

A humorless laugh slipped from his mouth.

"What?" Kate asked.

"Let's just say he tried to touch her in a way that a girl her age shouldn't be touched."

Kate's eyes narrowed. "What does that mean?"

"It happened about a week before Craig's death. Debbie came over to talk to Craig and . . . I don't know; you said Craig knew he had a brain tumor and wasn't going to live . . . Maybe he wasn't thinking straight. Maybe he thought he had nothing to lose. She liked him, she was pretty—"

"Stop," Kate said through clenched teeth. "I will not sit here and listen to this garbage."

"But don't you see? That's what caused the falling out between them. That's why Ricky fired him, and that's why he hates me and our family. I saw Ricky at the cemetery and he said he felt sorry for any children I had. Now I know what he meant, and I don't blame him for saying it."

"There's no way . . . He couldn't . . ." Kate covered her mouth. "Andy . . . no—"

"Look," he said, "there's no way we can know exactly what happened. Nate only overheard bits and pieces through an open window as he was walking past. But there's no reason Nate would make this up. He didn't even want to tell me. I almost wish he hadn't told me, because now . . ."

"What?"

"Because now I can't stop wondering why Ricky didn't tell anyone. If we go on the assumption this really happened, why didn't Ricky go to the police?"

"A victim is a victim," Kate answered. This was something she had learned as a teacher. "It doesn't matter what kind of crime; the victim still feels shame and feels they did something wrong."

"But Ricky wouldn't feel that way. He'd be plenty upset about it. No, I think there's more to it than that. You have to remember this is a small town. Word spreads in a small town."

"What are you saying? That Ricky didn't want anyone to know?"

"Just think about it for a second. Craig worked for Ricky. Ricky took him under his wing, invited him into his life . . . and this was how Craig repaid him? How would that look to everyone else? It would make Ricky look like an idiot. A fool."

"Do you really think Ricky cares what other people think?"

"I think it's a possibility. Maybe not the right one, but it's a strong one. Or . . ."

"Or what?"

"Ricky strikes me as the type of man who keeps his business to himself. And takes *care* of it by himself."

At first she didn't understand what he was getting at; then all at once it sank in. "Andy, are you really suggesting—"

"Don't you think it's odd that Craig just happened to die shortly after that, and in such a bizarre way? It all fits. Craig tries to molest Debbie, Debbie tells her grandfather, grandfather gets mad, kills Craig, makes it look like an accident."

Kate tried to speak but nothing came out. For an instant she actually found herself considering this possibility, but she quickly found a hole to punch through it.

"But what about the game?" she countered. "You're convinced Craig set it up before he died, based on the idea that he *did* commit suicide and knew exactly when he was going to die. But if Ricky killed him, then Craig couldn't be the one doing this. That means it has to be someone else."

"But who's to say Craig didn't already have the game set up before Ricky killed him?"

Kate frowned. "If you're going down that road, then maybe Aunt Mary is a part of it. And Debbie. And your buddy at the gas station. Maybe the whole town is in on it. Is that what this is, Andy? A massive Mortom conspiracy?"

"I don't know," he said irritably. "I'm just talking out loud, okay? I'm just saying there's more to the story, and Ricky *has* to be involved somehow. I'm sure of it. But I still think the game is from Craig. I still think he's the one doing this to me."

The question *why* sprang to her lips and she held it back—they had been over this before. They were treading water again.

"You were gone a while," Andy said. "What happened to you?"

Again she hesitated, trying to decide what to disclose. "I stopped at the courthouse in Keota."

"What for?"

"It had nothing to do with your stupid game. I just wanted to see if I could find Craig's birth record."

"Birth record," he repeated. Something seemed to dawn on his face. "Shit . . . on . . . me."

Kate's chest tightened. "What?"

"What if all this time we've been after the same thing without even realizing it? What if everything is connected?"

She recrossed her arms, unsure where this was headed and already not liking it.

Andy said, "What if *Ricky* is Craig's father?"

"No," she warned, shaking her head. "Don't even—"

"Just hear me out, okay? Because if that was the case, Craig would have been Debbie's uncle, and now we're talking incest. That'd be enough to send *anyone* over the edge."

"Are you really trying to tell me that Craig would try and get . . . try to *do* something inappropriate with his own niece?"

"But Craig didn't know," Andy said, his voice rising. "He had no idea, because Craig didn't know who his father was."

"But Mary said she told Craig about his father. He asked and she told him weeks before."

"But we don't know *what* Mary told him. There's only one way to find out."

Kate held out a hand as he stood. "Where are you going?"

"To see Mary."

"Like hell! Andy, you can't just march over there and ask something like that. Craig's father has nothing to do with you."

"If it has something to do with this game, then it has everything to do with me."

"And you've been drinking. And now you're going to drive?"

Andy considered. "You're right. It's a beautiful night for a walk."

"Andy, please—"

"I will not be rude, and I will not be crass. I simply have a few questions. You're the one wanting to know about the father, not me. And like you said before, part of what we're trying to do is figure out whether or not Craig's death was a suicide. Remember that from before, or was that all bullshit?"

He was changing things around again, mixing up the point. She didn't trust herself to speak.

"I want to figure out the game," he said, "and you want to know some things about Craig. Mary is the key. She *has* to have some answers. We both want different things, but we can help each other. You have to see that. It's all connected in some way or another. Can't we help each other?"

"Do you practice this shit in front of a mirror?" she asked in disgust.

"Is that a yes?"

She stared at him. "Fine. I'm going with you and I'll drive. You ask your stupid questions, and if you do it in a shitty way, I will drag you out of her house. I swear as God as my witness. I will drag you out and kick the crap out of you."

He chuckled. "You're kind of a tough broad. When you talk like that, I know you feel it, too."

"Feel what?"

"The excitement," he said, eyes glistening. "Come on, you lead the most boring life in the world. Isn't all this kind of exciting? It's a mystery and we're on an adventure. Twists and turns at every corner, pieces of a puzzle every step of the way."

"What happened to the fear?" she asked angrily. "The fear of Friday and thinking something bad will happen? Was that all bullshit? This really is no more than a game for you, isn't it?"

"Whatever happens, *happens*. I'm ready for it now. I'm tired of being scared, Kate, tired of running from things. I'm going to meet this head on. If I die, at least I die with my sense of humor intact."

"That's not funny."

His face sobered. "Sorry."

"Let's go before I change my mind."

She started for the door and he moved in front of her. "One last thing. All joking aside."

"What?"

"I promised Nate I wouldn't repeat what he told me. I wouldn't have told you under normal circumstances, but considering our circumstances are anything but normal . . ."

"Yeah, I get it."

"Will you be okay with her?"

She scowled. "With who?"

"With Debbie. I know how you are, Kate. The next time you see her you'll probably try to get her to open up and spill everything that happened."

"I don't want to talk about her with you," she said. "Let's just get this over with."

Andy looked after her. "That's what I thought."

29

Mary was sitting on the porch with a coffee mug in one hand and a crossword in the other. She scarcely glanced up as the two of them came up the lawn.

"I'm kind of busy now," she said. "Got to finish this puzzle and then put away my laundry."

Andy lifted the crossword from her hand. "We'll be quick."

"What is this, the third degree or something? Both of you standing there, looking at me like I did something wrong. You best go away. I'm not in the talking mood."

"You said something to Kate about Craig's father," Andy said. "Back at the house."

"Craig's daddy was nobody. Just some guy I knew and dated for a short time. We dated and then he died. There's nothing more."

Andy and Kate exchanged a glance.

"I was confused," Mary went on. "Sometimes I talk nonsense and don't realize it. It doesn't mean anything. Just bad medication or something."

"Is Ricky Simms the father?" Andy asked in a strong voice.

Mary looked like she had been slapped. "Ricky Simms is a monster, and I would have drowned Craig at birth if he'd had any hand in making him. I have nothing but contempt for the man, just a little more than I'm having for the two of you right now."

"I'm sorry," Kate said. "We're not trying to upset you."

"Then leave. And don't come back anymore. I've already had words with your mother today and she wasn't happy."

Kate's stomach rolled. "You talked to Mom?"

"She called a bit ago, wanting to know about all this daddy nonsense. I told her you were bothering me and it was very upsetting."

"Mary," Kate began, "I—"

Her words broke off as the screen door banged open. The man holding the knob was built like a linebacker and looked just as friendly. Both arms were inked with tattoos, and the red bandana across his forehead was set so low his eyes were barely visible.

"Is there a problem, Mare?" he asked.

"No problem, Billy. My niece and nephew were just leaving."

To Kate's relief Andy retreated toward the pickup; apparently there was still *some* common sense rattling around inside him.

"I'm sorry," Kate said again to Mary. "Sorry."

She made her way to the pickup and climbed inside. "Thanks for making things worse."

Andy's gaze was fixed on the porch. "Remember the phone call I got at the house? It was a man's voice, and it sounded like a *big* guy—"

"I don't want to hear it. What was I thinking coming here with you?"

"You were supposed to stop me from pissing her off, remember? I don't think it worked."

Kate shook her head. "I can't even talk to you right now."

"They're still on the porch," Andy said in a low voice. "I don't know what Mary's saying, but there's a heap of words dropping from her mouth. And what's with this guy, anyway? Mary easily has fifteen years on him. This means something. That guy is involved in this, without a doubt. I need to get back and talk to Nate. Nate will know something."

"Andy, let's just go."

"You're the one in the driver seat. Drive."

"No," she said, "I mean *leave*. Back to Luther, right now. We'll go to the house, pack our things, and head home."

"We better go somewhere, because in about two seconds Mary's boyfriend is going to come over and chew us out or chew us up."

Kate leaned forward and saw Billy staring at them with his hands balled at his sides. Whatever Mary had told him, he hadn't liked it.

"Yeah," Kate said, stomping on the gas. "I think we're in agreement on that."

"Drop me off at the house and take the truck," he told her. "Go back home if you want. I'll find a way to Luther when I'm ready."

"Just like that, huh?"

"Unlike you, I can't just leave. You're obviously forgetting about the Friday deadline."

"No, Andy, I'm not. *Unlike* you, I don't think anything is going to happen come Friday."

"That's your opinion," he said mildly.

"Fine. Let's just say it isn't all bullshit. It's pretty obvious you expect to find money at the end of all this, right?"

He didn't answer.

"Well?" she asked. "Am I wrong? Maybe Craig left you his private collection of rare and expensive oil paintings. Or maybe he boxed up all those valuable, priceless statues he had sitting around the house. Or maybe—"

"Okay," he said crossly, "you've made your point. Not that it matters, but yes . . . I think it's money."

"Cash, right? Cold, hard currency, bundled in twenties and fifties?"

"Why is that so hard to believe, Kate? Craig had nothing in his savings account. There was nothing in his checking account. Don't you think it's a little suspicious that his estate and debt basically cancel each other out?"

"No. Craig had massive credit card debt and empty bank accounts because he was horrible with money. He worked part-time in a cemetery and did God only knows what else to pay his bills. But you're telling me, somehow—some *way*—he managed to hoard a pile of cash to leave behind for you . . . but only if you play some insane game to find it."

"Yes."

She looked at him and realized he was serious. "But why? Why would he go to all this trouble?"

"Look, I don't expect you to understand. It goes back to the thing we had between us. The competition. The money's there, but I have to work for it. And if I can outsmart him, he feels I deserve it."

"And what if there's nothing? What if in the end all you find is a piece of paper that says, 'Ha-ha.'"

He shrugged. "Then I'll know."

"But at what cost, Andy? This game has already brought out the worst in you. How far are you willing to go?"

"In case it's not obvious, I'm not in the best financial position these days. I'm unemployed and divorce lawyers aren't cheap. If there's a chance I can find some cash by doing nothing more than indulging my weirdo cousin, so be it."

"And how much money will it be, Andy? A million dollars? Fifty thousand? Five hundred?"

Andy said nothing.

Kate said, "If you're having money problems, I can loan—"

"No thanks," he replied tersely.

"I forgot; take nothing from anyone, right? Everyone's business and problems are their own. Fine. But think about this: instead of wasting the last three days with this nonsense, you could have been back in Luther looking for a job, or even playing the lottery. That's saner than this."

"The lottery is luck," he said. "This is skill."

She made herself stop. If he didn't give a shit about his lot in life, then why should she? The only reason she was still in Mortom was for Aunt Mary. If not for that, she would have already driven back to Luther. But there was no way she could leave now, not with everything that had happened.

Somehow, she had to make things right.

30

The phone inside Craig's house began to ring the moment Andy was out of the truck, and he almost knocked Kate down in his scramble up the steps. This time he would recognize the voice if it belonged to Mary's new friend.

"Hello?" he answered. "Who is this?"

"What in God's name is going on down there?"

His brow softened. "Mom?"

"Mary just called me. She said you and Kate were over again, badgering her about Craig's father. What are you doing to that poor woman?"

"Nothing," Andy said evenly. "Someone is doing something to us—"

The phone thumped in his ear.

"Mom?"

A new voice spoke up. "Andrew?"

It was his father. Now he was going to get answers.

"What's going on, Dad?" he asked. "Why is everyone freaking out about Craig's father? Was he a convicted felon or something?"

"I don't know what you're trying to accomplish, but it stops here and now. You know better than this."

Heat flooded his cheeks. "All I'm trying to do—"

"Mary doesn't talk about Craig's father, and we don't ask about Craig's father. If you have no respect for your aunt, then at least have some respect for your mother and knock this shit off."

The phone went dead. Andy slammed it down and turned on Kate. "Now Dad's pissed off . . . Why couldn't you just stay out of it?"

Her mouth dropped. "You're blaming me for this?"

"You're the one that started all this father crap. Everything was fine before you butted in."

"Everything was *not* fine, and you jumped on board the second you realized it could affect your stupid game! Unlike you, I was trying to help Mary."

"She doesn't want your help!" he shouted. "*I* don't want your help! Why can't you figure that out? This isn't a classroom and we're not a bunch of five-year-olds!"

"What's *that* supposed to mean?"

"Some of us have real problems, Kate, real things to deal with. Your biggest worry is trying to choreograph nap time and snack time so it doesn't interfere with reading time. It must be nice."

She stared at him through cold eyes. "You're an asshole."

"You're right," he laughed. "I'm an asshole. After all these years you've finally figured me out. So go bother someone else now for a while, okay? Call up some old boyfriends and remind them how messed up they are, because it was always them and never you, right? It couldn't be you, because everyone *loves* to be nagged at nonstop."

"You don't even know what you're saying anymore," she said, moving toward the staircase.

"Oh, but I do, Kate. Because that's what it takes to make you feel better about your own empty life, doesn't it? Nothing beats the feeling of putting someone in their place—"

"Go to hell!" she shouted.

"Yeah? Well, I'll be sure to say hi to our child-molesting cousin for you while I'm there!"

She stormed down the stairs and slammed the front door.

"I don't need you," Andy said to the empty room. "I don't need anyone."

31

Kate sat on the front step, watching the sun slip away into the horizon. The air had turned cool and she could hear the faint sounds of wind chimes in the distance. It was so easy to just sit there and watch the world as it moved around her. No worries or cares. To do nothing. Be nothing.

She closed her eyes and imagined herself back in Luther, curled up on her couch, watching television, dozing in and out of sleep. The alarm clock would be set for nine, because she wouldn't want to sleep away the day. Oh no. There were books to read, laps to swim, and bike trails to explore. And ice cream to eat. Lots and lots of ice cream—

"Are you okay?"

Kate opened her eyes. Debbie was standing at the edge of the driveway with her hands shoved into her pockets.

"Hi," Kate said, wiping her cheeks and realizing they were damp. "Sorry, I was . . . woolgathering."

"That's like spacing off during class, huh?"

Kate smiled. "Pretty much."

"I'm sorry."

"It's okay. You're not bothering—"

"Grandpa doesn't want me to talk to you," Debbie said. "And now I have to sneak over when he's gone because he hates you. He hates you and it's because of me."

Kate tried to swallow but all the saliva was gone from her mouth. "I'm sure he doesn't *hate* us. He just doesn't know us."

"It's my fault. All this bad stuff is because of me."

"Debbie, if something . . . *bad* happened and you want to talk about it, you can trust me. We're friends."

"You barely know me."

"That doesn't matter. I know you're a good person."

"Don't say that." Debbie's voice had gone tight. "You don't know anything about me. And tomorrow or the next day you'll be gone and you won't even think about this place again."

"That's not true."

"You don't know," Debbie whispered. Her eyes were wide, ready to fill with tears. Her feet began to propel her backward. "I need to get back."

"Wait!"

Debbie took off across the street. A noise turned Kate's head, and she saw Andy at the screen door.

"Go away," she snapped.

He lingered for a moment, eyes on hers, before retreating up the staircase.

"To hell with you," she said. "And to hell with Craig."

She sat there feeling miserable and alone, wishing she had never come to Mortom.

32

Midnight.

Andy sat in a half crouch, listening to the rustling of the trees. The shed was no more than a black shape in the distance, but he didn't dare use the flashlight until he was inside. More than one night of his youth had been wasted binge drinking in cemeteries, and he had no doubt the practice was still in use today. Of course, kids today were more apt to be vandalizing headstones or dealing drugs. He was probably more likely to get shot than reported to the police.

He gave the cemetery a final sweep before crossing the road. The urge to rush was almost overwhelming, and he forced himself to move slowly as he passed through the open gate. The half-mile walk to the cemetery had been anything but fun, and he couldn't imagine trying to make his way back on a twisted ankle.

As if on cue his foot discovered a sinkhole, and he caught himself on a headstone before falling on his face.

"Stupid," he hissed.

He brushed off his hands. Everything about this was stupid. He was a grown man, creeping around a cemetery in the middle of the night, on a treasure hunt with a key he wasn't sure was going to work. He needed to have his head examined.

He started moving again, this time using the headstones for balance. A branch snapped in the distance, and he slowed his step, tracking the darkness for any signs of movement. A squirrel or rabbit, that was all. If he started jumping at every sound, he was going to give himself a coronary.

He took the key ring from his pocket as he reached the shed. For the briefest of an instant he found himself wishing he had never found it. It was a pointless thought, and he pushed it out of his head as he slid the key into the lock. There was no turning back now.

The padlock snapped open. Two keys accounted for, one left to go. Whatever the last key opened, it had to be inside.

He raised the flashlight as he opened the door. The air inside the shed was thick with the smell of gas and oil, and his pulse kicked up a notch when he saw the riding lawnmower.

"Gotcha," he said under his breath.

The last key was obviously meant to lead him to the mower, so the only logical explanation was that the clue was hidden somewhere on it. Somewhere that wouldn't be seen. All he had to do was figure out where . . .

He knelt and examined the seat. The vinyl was worn and cracked in several places but otherwise intact. If something was hidden inside, it had arrived through some form of osmosis.

He unscrewed the gas cap and found only gasoline. That took care of the obvious places.

He worked through the metal frame with his fingers, addressing every nook and cranny. There was nothing.

"But you're a tricky bastard," he said, wiping beads of sweat from his brow. "And I don't give up."

He set the flashlight on the ground and felt underneath the mower deck, careful not to cut himself on the blade. There were only dried clumps of grass.

He stood and took a step back. The first key had led him to the cemetery; the next key led him to the shed; the last key led him to the mower . . . It was so straightforward it was almost *too* obvious. Everything pointed to the mower. Everything led to it. It was practically as if . . .

"X marks the spot," he whispered.

He grabbed the mower by the steering wheel. It began to move, slowly at first and then with more speed. He pulled it out the door and went back inside. The dirt beneath the mower was damp with oil, but the earth itself looked unbroken.

"It has to be."

He pushed up his sleeves and selected a hand shovel from the wall. If something was buried there, he prayed to God it wasn't going to be very deep.

33

Andy flicked away his cigarette and wiped a sweaty hand across his forehead as he looked at the sky. Clouds were forming overhead, and he was pretty sure he had heard the faint booms of thunder in the distance more than once. The last thing he needed was a storm; that would only bring a muddy mess. He already had enough of a mess on his hands.

He shone the flashlight beam into the shed and glowered at the hole in the dirt. Two feet down and nothing. A total waste. No, that wasn't exactly right—he had managed to dig a hole that was going to be noticed the first time the mower was moved. The worst part was he was right back where he had started: nowhere. The mower was the only thing in the shed that took a key, so what was he missing? God forbid he would need to take the stupid thing apart, bolt by bolt.

He sat on the seat and examined the key ring for the umpteenth time. The big key was for the gate that led into the cemetery. The next key opened the shed. That left the small key, which had to go to the mower. It didn't get much more formulaic than that.

"Maybe I am supposed to drive you," he said. "Drive you right off a cliff with me on it. How about that, huh? That would show 'em. That would end all this mess."

He halfheartedly put the key to the ignition, doubting the stupid motor would turn over, let alone start. The mower looked like it hadn't run in years.

The key slid in halfway and stopped.

He pulled it out with a frown. The tip looked slightly bent, but other than that it looked fine. He tried again, this time with more force. Again it stopped halfway, refusing to mesh with the tumblers inside. It was almost as if—

"Son of a bitch," he said quietly.

The key didn't fit.

And that meant the key opened something else.

He swept the beam of light around the shed, first to the bags of fertilizer in the corner, then to the tools on the wall. He moved the beam to the shelf above the door. It was littered with random junk: a cracked football helmet, handlebars to a bicycle, a rusty bucket . . . The last item was some sort of metal, oval container. It was covered with a thin layer of dust, but the dust was streaked in several places, as if it had been recently disturbed.

He wet his lips as he reached for it. In his mind's eye he could visualize Craig doing the same: reaching over his head, grasping the object with both hands, carefully lifting it down. It took less than a second for his mind to process what he was holding (he had been the proud owner of one in college) but the gas tank on *his* motorcycle had been attached to the actual motorcycle—not sitting on a shelf, collecting cobwebs.

And like his motorcycle, this gas tank had a key lock.

He set the tank on the ground and took out the small key. It slid effortlessly into the lock, and the cap snapped open. No gasoline was inside, but there was something else.

He turned over the tank and gave it a shake. A tiny audiocassette, no bigger than a small box of matches, clattered out onto the floor.

He stared at it without blinking. Every clue up until this point had been written, and even though the handwriting seemed to match Craig's, there was no way to be absolutely certain. But this . . . this was going to change all that, because he had no doubt—absolutely none—that when he played this tape, he was going to hear a voice. And when he heard that voice . . .

He studied on this carefully, not wanting to rule out any options. If the voice on the tape *wasn't* Craig, that still didn't mean Craig wasn't involved. Craig could have easily written something down and had someone else read it. Why? To throw him off track, of course. To mess with his head. But whom would Craig get to do something like that? It would have to be someone he trusted, but Craig had no friends. The only one that came close was—

"Ricky," Andy finished aloud.

This entire time he had been adamant about believing the game was from Craig, but what if Craig and Ricky Simms were in it together? Had he seriously never considered the possibility before?

He shifted uneasily as the thought tried to take root. If the two of them really were working together, how did the whole "falling out" thing fit in? Did it happen because of the game? Or maybe the game had already been set, and then the incident with Debbie took place, and that was when it happened? That seemed the most likely. Or . . .

"Or maybe it never happened at all?"

What if the falling out had been faked? What if it hadn't happened, but everyone was supposed to *believe* it had?

He cast his mind back and tried to sort his information. Kate was the one who had told him about the falling out, and she had gotten that information from Debbie. Debbie told Ricky that Craig tried to touch her, and that information had come from Nate, who (supposedly) overheard the conversation. Inasmuch as it was logical to believe the falling out had occurred because of Craig trying to touch Debbie, there was no way to know for sure. But if the falling out had been faked, where did that leave Nate in the whole mess? Because that meant Nate was lying, or Nate really *had* overheard the conversation . . . but it had been staged for his benefit. And that made no sense. That would be too convenient and coincidental. Almost as coincidental as everything else that had happened.

"Especially something like Craig having a brain tumor that no one knew about."

Kate had taken it at face value, but Andy had immediately thought it sounded suspicious. A little too cut-and-dried, a perfect excuse for Craig to take his life. And come to think of it, who was to say there really *had* been a tumor? With Craig gone, there was no way to verify this information. Papers could be faked; people could lie. But wouldn't that mean Mary was also involved?

"You don't know that," he said. "You don't even know what's on the tape."

He closed his fist around the cassette. He couldn't even think straight anymore. One thought led to another, and then he was ten steps away from where he had first started. The game was grinding him down, pitting himself against everything and everyone. In the back of his head he heard Kate's voice: *How far are you willing to go?*

How long could he keep this up? How many clues were there? Ten? Twenty? It could take weeks to unravel them all.

"And you have until Friday," he reminded himself.

All at once it felt like the temperature inside the shed had risen twenty degrees and pushed through the door and moved outside. A quick cigarette was what he needed to clear his head. He would smoke, clean up the mess inside, and head back to the house. First thing in the morning he would track down a miniature tape player, or try to find the one that Craig had used—

His cigarette stopped halfway to his mouth. There had been a sound from across the cemetery, almost like a faint cough.

He closed the shed door, blocking off the light from inside. His eyes scanned the surrounding darkness. If there had been someone, they were gone now. Probably just kids walking past on the road. Still, it was a good reminder to keep things moving. He had been lucky so far, but luck always ran out.

He went back inside the shed and picked up the hand shovel. It took less than a minute to push the dirt back into the hole, and when it was done it looked absolutely horrible. There was no way it would go unnoticed. Maybe Ricky would think squirrels had tried to burrow under the mower.

He returned the hand shovel to its hook and placed the motorcycle tank back on the shelf. Everything else seemed to be in place. All that was left was the mower.

He propped open the door and gave the area another quick glance. There was a tiny, orange light in the distance that hadn't been there before. It was no more than a speck, rising and falling through the air, fading and growing, almost like . . .

Fear leapt inside him: it looked like the tip of a lit cigarette.

He watched the dot as it continued to move. He told himself it was a lightning bug; it was a reflection off something . . . It was *anything* but *that*. Because if he allowed himself to believe it was a cigarette, then he had to accept that someone was holding it.

And that meant someone was standing there, watching him.

He latched on to the mower with both hands and quickly pulled it inside the shed. The flashlight was on the ground, still lit, and he shoved it deep into his pocket to diminish the light. He stood behind the door, breathing heavily, his mind racing. If it truly was someone—which it *wasn't*—what could he do about it? March over and confront them? More likely than not, it was just a teenager out sneaking a smoke.

And if that was the case, the best thing was for each of them to mind their own business. No harm, no foul.

He cracked open the door and peered out. The dot was still there, hovering in the darkness.

He stepped out, shut the door, and snapped the padlock into place. Now all he had to do was walk back into town.

Alone and in the dark.

The orange dot blinked out.

WEDNESDAY

34

Kate rolled over and opened her eyes. The clock by the bed said it was almost noon, but her body insisted it had to be earlier. Her arms and legs felt as if they had been dipped in wet cement, and it was a struggle to open her eyes more than half-mast. The worst was her stomach: her insides felt like they had been sucked clean by a high-powered vacuum cleaner. Not that that was a surprise; she couldn't begin to count how many times she'd been jarred awake during the night to dry heave over the toilet. Whatever was in her system seemed to have no intention of vacating anytime soon.

She mounted the staircase and braced herself for her brother. Shortly before midnight she had heard him sneak out, and she had no doubt he had gone to the shed with the keys he had found. He was going to get himself hurt or arrested if he kept this up, and unfortunately there was no one but her to keep an eye on him. Left to his own devices he might burn down the town or rob a liquor store . . . provided he found a note telling him to do so.

She stopped with a frown at the top of the staircase. The living room was empty, and Andy's shoes weren't in sight, which meant he hadn't slept on the couch last night. He never took off his shoes until the moment he went to bed, and even then they were always within a few feet, as if he might have to leap up in the middle of the night and rush out the door. He had been that way since high school.

She went to the living room window and saw the pickup in the driveway.

"Andy?" she called out.

She checked the bathroom and felt a prick of unease when she found it empty. Her momentary fear was replaced by anger when she found him in Craig's room, fully clothed and asleep in Craig's bed.

"Are you kidding me?" she shouted.

He bolted upright and looked around, dazed. "I'm awake."

"What the hell are you doing?"

"Could you please not yell?" he asked, touching his forehead. "What time is it?"

"That's all you have to say? What *time* is it?"

He staggered to the closet and pulled down a shirt. "Can you at least tell me if it's before noon?"

"This is sick, Andy."

"I found the next clue."

"I said—"

"I heard what you said," he snapped. "Do we really have to have an argument two seconds after I wake up?"

Kate's mouth dropped. "You're sleeping in Craig's bed! You're wearing his clothes! How can you be so disrespectful?"

"It's all mine now. I can live how I want."

"*Live?* You barely eat, you don't shower . . . All you do is obsess. And you're drinking. You never drink."

"Two days," he said. "Two days and it'll all be over. Then we can all go back to our regular, miserable lives. I'm not going to fight with you, Kate. You're not Mom and you're not my wife. I don't have to answer to you. I can do what I want."

"Not when it affects our family."

"Hey, I didn't drag you to this town—"

"You asked me to come!" She hated him at that moment, more than she had ever hated anyone in her life. "I came here for you."

"Bullshit," he said, pointing a finger at her. "You came here because you felt guilty for skipping out on the funeral."

"I was laid up in bed with food poisoning! Unlike you, I didn't have a choice. *You* skipped because you didn't give a shit. You're only here now because there's something in it for you."

He laughed and pulled on his shoes. "Yep, I'm just an asshole. We've covered this ground before, remember? I'm sure you would have handled the situation with such grace and ease it would have made Mom and Dad proud."

She followed him into the hallway and down the staircase. "That's not the point and you know it."

"And what is the point, Kate? Please, enlighten me. Because I sure as hell don't know what you expect me to do or say anymore."

"We're supposed to be here for Aunt Mary."

"No, you're here for Mary. I'm here trying to figure out what Craig wants from me. So as much as I'd love to continue this conversation, I now have to go buy a tape player for the cassette I found last night. But will I be able to find one in Mortom? Of course not, because Craig probably took it upon himself to buy them all up and bury them, just to make my life more difficult. So I'm off to Keota to waste more time and try to figure out what I'm supposed to do next."

He went out the door. She opened her mouth to shout something after him—*anything*—and realized there was nothing to be said. She was out of words.

He gave her a two-finger salute as he climbed into the pickup, and she watched as he backed out and almost hit the mailbox before heading down the road.

"Good riddance," she mumbled.

Movement caught her eye across the street, and she ducked back as Ricky's pickup rolled out of the garage and took off in the same direction. It was a heck of a coincidence, and she might have been more concerned if Debbie wasn't standing at the door, watching him go. Ricky was Andy's worry; Debbie was hers.

She went to the kitchen, found the casserole dish that had been washed and forgotten, and carried it across the street. Debbie appeared at the door before Kate had a chance to knock.

"You shouldn't be here," she said.

Kate held up the dish. "I only came to return this."

"I don't believe you."

"I also wanted to make sure you were okay. You ran off so fast last night."

"I'm not supposed—"

"To talk to me. I know. I'm not here to make trouble for you. You know that, right?"

Debbie cracked the screen and took the dish. "Thanks."

"But I really would like to talk. Just one minute and then I'll leave. I promise."

"I don't know when Grandpa will be back. Sorry."

"Well, can I at least get some antacid pills? My stomach has really been bothering me—"

"Sorry."

The screen started to close and Kate stopped it with her hand.

"You're scared," Kate said quietly. "I get that. I can only imagine what it must be like to be a young girl, away from home, and stuck in a small town without anyone to confide in. Believe it or not, sometimes it's easier to talk to someone you don't know very well. Sometimes that's the only thing that makes sense."

Debbie dropped her eyes and fidgeted with the dish. Kate released the screen.

"I'm sorry," she said.

"Do you really need something for your stomach?"

"I really could use something, yeah."

Debbie checked the street again, then Kate's eyes. She nodded. "Okay."

She disappeared inside. Kate lingered at the door, unsure whether she was supposed to wait or follow, and then stepped inside. Debbie was rummaging through a drawer by the stove. Kate sat at the table. A row of cookbooks lined the wall, and one had a photograph sticking halfway out. She wiggled it out a few inches and saw a very young Ricky Simms standing alongside a woman with stark black hair. Neither was smiling.

"Here," Debbie said, handing her the pills.

"Is this your grandma?"

"We called her Nans. She's been gone for three years now. She died of cancer."

"I'm sorry."

"Grandpa could barely function after that. It really worried Dad. Sometimes when one old person dies, the other gets so depressed they die, too. Have you heard that?"

"Your grandpa seems like he's got a pretty strong will. I bet he'll be around for a long time to come."

"That's when I started coming here. It seemed to help. Grandpa also really liked having Craig around . . ."

She trailed off. Kate realized she was still holding the antacid pills and popped them in her mouth.

"He used to pretend to be homeless," Debbie said. "Did you know that?"

"Your grandpa?"

"Craig. We heard Mr. Bassett telling his wife how Craig would dress like a bum and beg for money in Keota. I guess he did it a lot."

Kate held back a frown. It was no secret Craig had been eccentric, but she had no idea it ran that deeply. She realized again how little she knew about her cousin.

"Grandpa heard that and laughed," Debbie said. "It was the first time he had laughed since Nans died. He thought it was the funniest thing ever. 'Beating the system' he called it. The next time he saw Craig he started talking to him. Isn't that funny? They lived across the street for years but never talked. Craig kept to himself, and Grandpa isn't the friendliest person in the world. But he really did like Craig. And Craig liked him. And I . . . I messed it all up."

"Debbie, it wasn't your fault."

"It was." Tears filled her eyes. "You don't know."

Kate reached out and took Debbie's hand . . . and all at once believed. It was true. Craig was a monster.

"Debbie, listen to me. Sometimes people make mistakes. *Horrible* mistakes. Sometimes they do it on purpose, but sometimes they can't help themselves. Does that make sense?"

"I guess so . . ."

"Sometimes," Kate said softly, "people do things because they can't help it. Like . . . like when you're sick and have a cold. You have to blow your nose, right? You can't control that. And sometimes people are sick in other ways, and they can't control what they do. Or things get messed up in their head . . ."

She struggled with what to say. Now she was going to make excuses for Craig?

"Craig was sick in the brain with a tumor. Do you know what that is?"

Debbie began to cry. "Yes."

"You can tell me anything," Kate said. "*Tell* me, Debbie."

"If I do . . . will you promise to go away and never come back? Because I think you're going to hate me after I tell you."

Kate squeezed her hand. "I won't hate you."

"Craig told me about the tumor. I was at his house, and it was beautiful outside, and I was in a really good mood . . . and just like that, he said he was going to die, just like Nans. I started to cry. He hugged me . . . and . . ."

Debbie let out a wracking sob.

"What?" Kate asked. Her heart was thundering inside her chest. "What happened then?"

"I . . . told him . . . I was in love with him."

For a moment Kate was so taken aback she wasn't sure she had heard correctly. "You told Craig that you *loved* him?"

"I knew you'd think it was stupid," Debbie said, pulling away. "Just like he did."

"No," said Kate. "I didn't—"

"He laughed! He said it was just a crush, and a girl my age doesn't know anything about love!"

Kate sat there dumbfounded, trying to process what she was hearing.

"He tried to take it back when he saw how upset I was," Debbie said with a heavy sob, her voice wavering with anger. "But I wouldn't let him. It hurt me so bad I wanted to die. He kept trying to take it back . . . He said it didn't mean anything, but it *did* mean something. It meant everything. He hurt me, and . . . and . . ."

Kate covered her mouth.

"I was angry," Debbie said. "I ran here crying, and Grandpa wanted to know what was wrong, but I couldn't tell him. He would have laughed at me, too. Him and Craig would have sat on the porch and drank beer and laughed about it. Grandpa kept asking me and asking me . . . He knew I had been over at Craig's . . ."

Debbie's mouth continued to move, but nothing came out.

"Debbie," Kate asked carefully, "what happened then?"

"He . . . Grandpa asked if Craig did something to me. And I started nodding my head. I thought if I answered, he'd leave me alone. All I wanted was to be left alone. But he wouldn't. He kept asking me what happened . . . asking what Craig did . . . if Craig had . . . touched me . . ."

Kate felt a sick lump work its way up her throat.

"I kept nodding. I mean, Craig had touched me when we hugged . . . but deep down I think I knew what he was *really* asking . . . but it was just so easy to keep nodding my head. I was so mad at Craig I didn't care . . . He hurt me so bad . . . and all I wanted to do . . . all I wanted was to . . ."

"Hurt him back," Kate whispered.

"I wanted him to feel like I did," Debbie choked. "I didn't want them to laugh at me. And I knew it was wrong, but I couldn't take it back either. I couldn't!"

She wiped her eyes with her palms and shook her head.

"Craig came to the house to see if I was okay. Grandpa took out his shotgun and said he would shoot Craig if he came around again . . . and the whole time Craig kept looking at me because he was confused, and that only made Grandpa angrier, because he thought Craig wanted to hurt me for telling on him. And then Craig left and I never saw him again. And when we learned he died, Grandpa was happy. He said he was happy Craig was dead, and he deserved it. And it was because of me."

"Craig's death was an accident," Kate stammered.

"But what if it wasn't?" Debbie asked in a hushed voice. "What if Craig killed himself because of what I did?"

Debbie was staring at her with wide eyes, waiting for reassurance, waiting for Kate to make it better.

"Debbie . . ."

That was when they heard Ricky Simms's pickup pull into the driveway.

35

Andy had the cassette player free of its package before he was out of the store, and he almost dropped it twice because his hands were shaking so badly. By the time he climbed into his truck, his heart was hammering so violently he thought it was going to break free of his chest. His fingers fumbled with the batteries, trying to tear them from their plastic prison.

"Come on—"

The package flew open, scattering batteries throughout the cab. He snatched two from the floor, pushed them into the player, and slid the cassette inside.

His thumb hovered over the "Play" button as he took in a controlled breath. He needed to be calm, focused. Whatever was on the tape, he had to be ready.

He started the player and closed his eyes.

"So here we are," said the voice on the tape.

The shrill voice was familiar at once—Craig had never outgrown his prepuberty voice, even as a man.

"I'll cut right to the chase," Craig said. "So far I've been gentle, but playtime is over. The next clue changes everything. The good news is I'm going to tell you what it is. It's a book. A book very special to me called *Perdum*."

Andy stopped the tape and grabbed a pen from the glove box. He wrote the word on the back of his hand, committed it to memory, then started the tape again.

"All the answers are in the book," said Craig. "The trick is finding the book. Finding it will be a good trick indeed."

Andy let the tape run, waiting for more. There was nothing. He rewound it and listened to it again from the beginning.

"All the answers are in the book," he echoed.

It seemed too easy. Find the book and all the answers would be inside? All the answers . . .

He started the truck and rolled down the road in search of a book-store.

36

"What the Christ is this?" Ricky said, tossing his keys on the table. Kate saw none of this but heard everything: she was in the bathroom behind the closed shower curtain with one hand clamped across her mouth.

"The front door needs to stay shut," Ricky said. "I'm not paying to have the outside air-conditioned. And why are your eyes all red? Have you been crying again?"

"Allergies," Debbie said.

Kate stiffened as footsteps padded the hallway.

"Did you forget something?" Debbie asked. "I can get it for you."

"I can get my own checkbook, thank you very much." The footsteps passed by the bathroom. "I'm not as helpless as your father makes me out to be."

"I know." Debbie's voice was crisp and clear, just outside the door. "I was just trying to help."

More footsteps in the hallway.

"If you'll excuse me," Ricky said. "I have business."

Kate closed her eyes. He was leaving. All she had to do was stay collected for another few seconds—

"And put the toilet seat back up when you're done!" Ricky hollered.

Every muscle in Kate's body seized; Ricky was in the bathroom. He began to relieve himself, a slow trickle into the bowl.

"Easy now," he whispered.

The trickle picked up into a stream. Kate stood motionless, afraid to breathe.

"Have you been talking to that lady?" Ricky called out.

Debbie's voice was faint: "No."

"And if that man tries to talk to you? What then?"

"Shut the door and lock it. But—"

"You mind me," Ricky said. "You never used to talk back like this, and I won't stand for it."

The toilet flushed. A moment later she heard footsteps in the hallway and let out her breath in a giant whoosh.

"Stay in the house," Ricky's voice drifted back. "I don't want . . . Why do you keep looking down the hallway?"

Kate closed her eyes as her insides tried to claw up her throat.

"I . . . I'm not," Debbie stammered.

"Why are you acting so funny?" His voice was sharp. "What's going on?"

"Nothing!"

Kate was past the point of panic now, barely able to use her legs to support herself.

"You better come with me," Ricky said. "I need to go to Keota, and I don't want you here alone while I'm out of town."

"But—"

"Get your shoes on."

Silence.

"Come on now. You obey me."

After an eternity the front door opened and closed. When the pickup roared to life, Kate threw back the shower curtain and emptied her stomach into the toilet.

37

"*Perdum*," the woman repeated, pecking away at the keyboard. "Do you know the author?"

Andy shook his head. "Nope."

He drummed his fingers against the counter and glanced at the teenage boy and girl thumbing through the sex books in the corner. The girl caught him watching and went red in the cheeks.

"Here we go. *Perdum*, James Arthur Housel. Nineteen thirty-two."

"Great," he said, pulling out his wallet. "Do you take credit cards?"

"Nineteen thirty-two is the year it was published," she said, tapping again at the keyboard. "And the book is out of print."

"Of course it is," he said.

"I could try the distributor and see if they have any copies on hand. The only downside is it usually takes a few weeks."

"You're sure it's out of print?" he asked, trying to control his irritation. "Does that happen a lot?"

"Books by major authors have multiple print runs, but unless it's a bestseller, there's usually only one printing. Believe it or not, the majority of books lose money for the publisher. It's the nature of the business.

But like I said, I can certainly try and order you a copy. There's no extra charge."

"No," he said, heading for the door. "Thanks."

"You might try a used bookstore," she called after him. "Maybe—"

The door cut off her words as it closed behind him. How was he supposed to get his hands on something they didn't print anymore? He didn't have a few weeks; he didn't even have a few days.

He climbed into the truck and slammed the door in frustration. *All the answers are inside the book* . . . Even if he found it, what then? Read the book cover to cover, looking for clues? It was insanity.

He picked up the player and listened to the message again. "Tricky . . . all the answers . . . very special to me . . ."

"Very special," he repeated.

Maybe the tricky part wasn't tracking down *any* copy of the book, but rather a *specific* copy of the book, a copy Craig already owned. And once he found it, there would be something inside, like a slip of paper with instructions, or maybe something written on the pages. Maybe even a drawing or a map. That made more sense than trying to find a random copy.

He stared out the windshield, mulling over his next course of action. If it was a copy Craig already owned, that meant it was probably hidden at the house. But if it was hidden, why wouldn't Craig have given him clues to find it, like he had with all the other puzzles?

"Because it's not a puzzle," he said. "It's sitting on the bookshelf in plain sight."

But there was nothing tricky about that. Unless the "tricky" part was that there *wasn't* anything tricky about this clue . . .

He sat there, uncertain how to proceed. It came down to two choices: keep searching bookstores around Keota or drive back to Mortom. If the book wasn't at the house, he would end up back here searching. But if the book was sitting on the bookshelf at the house, searching here was only going to waste more time.

"It's inside the house," he said. "It has to be."

His fingers tightened around the steering wheel. The longer he sat there, the more time he wasted. He knew this. But that wasn't the real problem. The problem was that his brain was so taxed he could barely think anymore. He simply could not come to a decision. He couldn't make a choice.

He dug a quarter from his pocket. If this was what it had to come to, so be it. Heads, he would stay and keep searching. Tails, he would drive back to Mortom.

He flipped the coin and caught it in a fist. When he opened his hand, he saw the eagle staring back at him.

"Lucky bird," he whispered.

He stomped on the gas and started back toward Mortom.

38

Kate hurried down the staircase when she heard the pickup in the driveway, and waited for Andy at the door. The Simms house was still empty, and Kate could only hope that Debbie had kept herself together. If not . . . she didn't want to think about what could happen.

"I'm glad you're back," Kate began. "I—"

"Stop," he said. "It's already been a long, crappy day, and I can't deal with you right now."

"No," she said, shaking her head. "I'm not . . . I wasn't . . ."

He was already up the staircase. She went after him and found him at the bookcase.

"I'm just glad you're home," she said quietly. "That's all I was going to say."

"Sure," he said, examining the bottom row of books. "And I'm sure if I turn around I *won't* find you staring at me with your arms crossed."

She unlaced her arms. "All I need is one minute of your precious time so we can talk."

"*Talk*," he laughed. "That's a nice way to put it."

"What does that mean?"

"Your definition of 'talking' is bitching, nagging, or making a speech."

Kate started to cross her arms again and caught herself. "Andy, I'm serious. This is important."

"The only thing that's important right now is finding the book I'm looking for. It's called *Perdum*. So unless you've seen it—"

"Just listen, okay? I talked with Debbie. She made it up. Craig didn't do anything to her."

Andy pulled out a book, checked the cover, and slid it back into place.

"Andy, did you hear what I said?"

"Yeah, made it up. Have you seen any other books around the house? Maybe in the basement?"

"*Asshole!*"

"And here we go."

"Forget about your goddamn game and book for one minute and listen to my words. Debbie . . . made . . . it . . . up."

Andy gave an impatient grunt. "Made *what* up?"

"Craig didn't do anything to her. He never tried to touch her. She was upset and mad at him and made everything up. Her grandpa thinks it happened, but she lied. *Nothing happened.*"

Andy's forehead wrinkled as he nodded thoughtfully. "All right, then. That's something."

He moved past her into the kitchen.

"That's it?" she said. "That's all you've got to say?"

He opened the cupboard door above the fridge. "What do you want me to say?"

"Maybe that you give a crap? That you care our cousin didn't try and molest the neighbor girl?"

"I do, and that's great. But it doesn't change anything."

"How can you say that? This changes everything."

"No, Kate, it really doesn't. Craig is still dead. I still have to find this book. The deadline to finish this game is still coming. You always get so caught up in the details that you lose sight of the big picture."

"Big picture?" Her face twisted into a knot of anger. "I don't give a shit about your *big picture*. People need to know the truth, and the truth is that Craig didn't do anything. That's all that matters."

"Fine. Run across the street and tell Ricky your precious truth and see what happens."

"I plan to," she said curtly. "Why wouldn't I?"

"Well, let's see. First off, he hates us. Two, he won't talk to us. Three, even if he *would* talk to us, it's not like he would believe anything we'd say."

"And that's where you're wrong. You want to know why?"

"Enlighten me."

"Because he's not like you. *Unlike* you, he actually gives a shit about something in this world: Debbie. And if I went over there and told him I had important information that affected her, he'd listen. He'd listen because he'd see that I was there to help."

Andy raised his eyebrows. "Wow. I must say, you've certainly convinced me with that overwhelmingly compelling argument. And you also managed to get in a dig at me. Well played."

Kate crossed her arms and pressed her lips together.

"Oh, don't stop now," he said. "We're just getting started. So just for fun, let's say he does believe you. Where does that leave Debbie?"

"What do you mean?"

"What do you think he's going to say when he learns Debbie made the whole thing up? 'Don't worry about it'? 'These things happen'?"

"That's not the point—"

"Craig is *dead*. What Debbie did may have contributed to that. Ricky is already disgraced over what's happened. He feels betrayed. He severed ties with someone he treated like a son. How do you think he's going to feel when he learns it was all based on a lie? And from his own granddaughter?"

"But . . ." Kate's mouth opened and closed as she struggled with her words. "It wasn't . . . She didn't—"

"None of that matters now. What's done is done. I don't know about you, but I don't want to know what Ricky Simms is capable of. Do you really want his anger turned on Debbie?"

Kate's face grew dark. "Of course not."

"Then save your precious truth, Kate. Save it and bury it in the ground. Some things are better off buried. Trust me, I know."

He left her in the kitchen. She stood there, unsure whether she was more furious with Andy or herself. Was she really that stupid? Of course it would all come back on Debbie; how could she have thought otherwise? There was no way Ricky could know. No one could ever know.

"I'm an idiot," Andy said from the living room.

She reluctantly peered around the corner. She doubted this was an apology, but if it was, it was no surprise he would do it from another room while out of sight.

"Look what I found," he said, holding up a slip of paper. "A notice for an overdue book."

"So?"

"An overdue book from the *library*."

"Yeah?" she asked impatiently. "So what?"

He shook his head with a small laugh. "Don't worry about it. It's just more 'big picture' stuff. You wouldn't understand."

She glared at him as he jogged down the staircase. The front door opened and closed, and she went to the living room window and gave the pickup an indifferent glance as he sped off.

Her gaze shifted across the street. There was still no sign of Debbie or Ricky. She told herself there was nothing to worry about; everything was going to be fine.

"Just fine," she told herself.

It sounded like a lie, even to her ears.

39

He brought the truck to a stop in front of the library, knowing it was probably a waste of time but figuring it was worth a shot. He was still mostly convinced the book belonged to Craig, but checking here first was a better option than ripping down drywall and tearing up carpet at the house. He wasn't that desperate. Not yet, anyway.

The inside of the library was dim and quiet. He lingered in the entrance, waiting for a decrepit librarian to come hobbling out from the back.

"Anybody home?" he called out.

"Just us dust bunnies," replied a female voice with a laugh. "Be out in two hops."

He moved inside and started scanning the bookshelves. The books didn't appear to be alphabetized by last name or title, and he could only imagine what kind of filing system was in place. If any.

"And what have we here?"

Andy turned and saw a plump college-aged girl with heavy makeup and busy hair holding an armful of books.

"Hey," he said.

"Hello yourself," she grinned, coming up and violating his personal space by several inches. "I don't think I know you, and I know all the boys in town."

Andy resisted the urge to take a step back; the smell of perfume and cigarette smoke was almost overwhelming.

"Are you open?" he asked.

"Sure are. We don't see too many faces during the day, so we just turn on every other light. *Murder* on the eyes, but it sure saves money. Isn't that a hoot? Here we are in a library, and it's probably the worst place in town a body could come to read."

"That is a hoot," Andy agreed.

"So where you from, stranger?"

"I'm just visiting. I'm hoping you can help me. I'm looking for a book called *Perdum*. It's pretty old."

"Older than you?" she asked, cocking an eyebrow.

"It was written in the thirties."

The girl laughed. "You're definitely not from a small town, that's for sure."

"Sorry?"

"You're all business and no small talk. That's not like folks around here. Plus, most of the boys that come in are flirty as all get out, but not you."

Andy smiled. "My girlfriend doesn't like it when I flirt."

"Girlfriend, huh?" She let out a playful sigh. "Is it pretty serious, you and her?"

He lowered his eyes. "It's so serious it's not even funny. We already have fish together."

The girl's brow creased for a moment and then she broke into a laugh. "You're a funny guy, you know that?"

"So I've been told. Now about the book—"

"Okay, stranger. Come on this way."

He followed her to the counter. "Like I said, it's called *Perdum*."

"Before we spend too much time on this, I'm guessing you don't have a library card."

"I'm sure my aunt does. Can I check it out under her name?"

"Well, that would be breaking the rules, stranger. How would we know you didn't just come to our fine town to steal our books and leave?"

Andy leaned over the counter with a wide smile. "I'd bring it right back when I was done. I have an honest face, right? Call me Andy, by the way."

A half grin pushed up the girl's cheek. "Well, now we're getting somewhere. What's your auntie's name?"

He looked directly at her as he spoke, for no reason other than curiosity to her reaction. "Mary Moore."

The girl squealed with laughter. "Virgin Mary? No friggin way! She's your auntie?"

Andy frowned. "Virgin Mary—"

"Shit! Did you know Creepy Craig?"

Andy wasn't sure what to address first—the obvious fact that Craig was his cousin because Mary was his aunt, or all the wonderful nicknames his family had acquired.

"Why do you call her Virgin Mary?" Andy asked.

"Oh." Her cheeks flushed. "Don't get me wrong, she's okay and all that. In fact, I don't really know her . . ."

The girl dropped her eyes and started typing.

"You know," Andy said, lowering his voice, "I was always partial to calling her Scary Mary."

The girl fought back a laugh.

"So why Virgin Mary?" he asked.

"It wasn't me. I mean, I wasn't the one who made it up or anything. I guess it's because she used to date a lot or something. Sort of like, on the prowl for a man."

Andy raised his eyebrows.

"It's like calling a fat guy Slim," she said. "Sort of like a joke, you know? Saying the opposite of what's true. Shit, I can't believe I'm telling you this."

"And Creepy Craig? Did you know him well?"

"*Everybody* knew Craig. He was . . . well, he was sort of the town weirdo."

"Really? How so?"

"He was just weird."

"Did he go out at night and molest animals?"

The girl snorted. "Well, no."

"Did he run around town naked?"

"*No*," she laughed.

Andy shrugged. "Then in what way was he weird?"

She looked at him for a moment, trying to decide if she was being put on or not.

"I don't know," she finally said. "You should talk to my sister. They kind of dated."

"Really? Was it recently?"

"Maybe a year ago, but it wasn't for long. They only went out a couple times."

"What kind of things did she say about him?"

"Well, I remember her saying he was a bad kisser . . ."

Not exactly the type of information he was searching for.

"She also said he was real sensitive, and he'd get bent out of shape real easy. Like he took *everything* anyone said super personally."

"Did he ever try to hurt her? Get violent?"

"Oh, no. He was harmless. Just not right in the head, you know? Like something wasn't clicking. Sad, really."

A small silence settled between them. Andy met her eyes and she gave him an apologetic smile.

"So," he said. "Back to the book."

"*Perdum*, right?" Her fingers worked the keyboard. After a moment she flicked the screen with a long, red fingernail. "Found it."

"Great." Something was finally about to go his way. "What shelf can I find it on?"

"Actually, the computer shows it's not in our inventory anymore. It was probably checked out and never returned."

"Was it Craig, by chance?"

"Naw, some guy named David Edmond, and that was two years ago. The computer doesn't show any activity on the book before that. We may have even sold it."

"Sold it?"

"Oh, sure. Every few years we go through our inventory and get rid of old books to make room for new stuff." She pointed to the bin by the door. "We dump everything in there and sell them for a quarter. In fact, your auntie used to come in every few months and buy tons of them. Maybe she bought it. Wouldn't that be funny?"

"Hilarious."

"What's the book about, anyway?"

He gave her a mirthless smile. "Practical jokes from beyond the grave. Thanks for looking."

He escaped through the front door and lingered on the side-walk, trying to figure out what to do next. The odds of Mary buying that book had to be astronomical, and even if she had, what were the chances of it being the specific copy Craig was talking about? Still, asking Mary was something that hadn't crossed his mind, and it was better than randomly searching bookstores or ripping apart the house.

He pulled himself into the truck. The girl was watching him through the glass door, and he gave her a two-finger wave as he started the engine.

"Lost cause," he said under his breath.

The words hung in the air, and he realized he wasn't sure if he was speaking about the girl or himself.

He put the truck into gear and set out for Mary's.

40

Kate slipped a glance over her shoulder as she entered the grocery store, unable to shake the feeling of being watched. A week ago she would have chastised herself over such petty paranoia, but after the last few days she wasn't so quick to rule anything out. She could still close her eyes and hear Ricky asking Debbie why she kept looking down the hallway. That memory was going to be with her a *long* time.

"Excuse me," she asked a passing clerk, "can you tell me where the medicine would be?"

"Just down this aisle past the cereal."

"Thank you."

She dropped a hand to her stomach and walked down the aisle. The antacid pills had done nothing, and now she was feeling worse; her entire body felt like it had been hit by a car. The only thing that didn't ache was her toes, and even those were starting to tingle.

She turned the corner and found herself at a cooler filled with orange juice. Nothing had ever looked so good, and she debated downing half the bottle right then and there. Her craving for it was almost overwhelming.

"Does this need money?" asked a small voice.

She looked down and saw a boy holding a bag of chips almost as big as he was.

"I would think so," she replied with a smile.

"Sometimes my dad lets me get something if it's not a lot of money."

"And where's your dad now?"

"You're pretty. Are you married?"

Kate couldn't help but laugh. "Actually, I'm not. Are *you* married?"

The boy shook his head. "I'm only five."

"Then it's probably a good thing. And now that we've resolved that, should we go find your dad?"

"I guess. He gets lost a lot."

"What's his name?"

"Daddy," the boy said, and then giggled. "But sometimes I call him booger breath and he laughs."

"I bet," Kate said with a grin. "Can you tell me what he looks like?"

The boy pointed behind her. "Like him."

Kate turned and smiled at the guy with the concerned brow coming toward them.

"Thank you so much," he said. "I was standing there, ogling the cream cheese, and the next minute he was gone."

"We've been getting along famously, discussing everything from food to matrimony."

"I bet," he said, tousling the boy's hair. "The only thing Tyler likes to do more than wander off is talk, don't ya, buddy?"

"Don't you think she's pretty, Daddy?"

Kate looked away, embarrassed.

"Seriously," he said. "Thank you."

"Oh, don't mention it. I love kids and always wanted some. The timing just hasn't been right. Not to mention Mr. Right has never been right."

It hung oddly in the air, and an awkward silence fell as their eyes met.

"Well," he said, "I suppose we better keep moving. His mother gets . . . *excitable* if I'm more than a few minutes late dropping him off."

Kate nodded. "Understood."

"I'm Jake, by the way," he said, offering his hand.

"Kate."

"It was very nice meeting you, Kate. Maybe I'll see you around?"

"Not if I see you first," she said, and then immediately felt stupid for saying it. "Yeah, maybe."

"Bye," Tyler said.

She gave them a wave. Then they were gone, like all the other men in her life. Or as Andy was fond of saying, wham-bam-thank-you-ma'am. That was her life, all right: a never-ending series of brief encounters. It was almost funny. Almost.

She found the medicine in the next aisle and squatted to examine the shelves. Once she got her aches and pains figured out, *then* she would go back to analyzing and trying to fix her love life . . .

A frown creased her forehead as her eyes fell on the tampons. Two thoughts crossed her mind simultaneously: she had forgotten to bring her own tampons for the trip, and today was Wednesday. That meant she should have started her cycle two days ago. She had been so preoccupied with everything going on, it had completely slipped her mind.

She rose to her feet and told herself to stay calm. Being a couple days late didn't necessary mean anything—sometimes her period did change. And with her body being so out of whack, her cycle could have easily slowed or changed . . .

All at once an image of Todd's bathroom rolled into her head. She had been brushing her teeth, and he had come up behind her and pulled her sweatpants to the floor. Cheap and sleazy, over in a matter of seconds. The next day they had parted ways. That had been a little over three weeks ago.

"It can't be," she whispered.

All the nausea . . . all the aches . . .

There was no way she was pregnant.

41

Andy found Mary in her backyard, digging in the garden. When she saw him coming, she stabbed the shovel into the dirt and rose to her feet.

"What's your business today?" she asked. "Come to harass me more about Craig's dead daddy?"

"Actually, I wanted to apologize for being such an ass."

"I don't believe a word you say. My guess is you want something. I don't know what it is, and even if I did, I probably wouldn't give it to you. So you might as well turn right back around and leave."

"Mary, I really am sorry—"

"Like hell." She leveled her stare at him. "You're not sorry for one thing you've done in your life. You're a selfish man and you always have been. I'm embarrassed to be related to you, if you want to know the truth. Your mother is one of the kindest women on this earth, and how you came from her womb is beyond me."

"Come on," he said with a chuckle. "You don't mean that."

"Do you know how many times Craig cried in my arms because of you?"

"I don't think—"

"Yeah, you *don't* think. Not at all. You were always too busy picking at him or telling him nonsense stories."

"We were kids. All kids say stupid stuff."

"He was a fragile and complicated boy. Do you have any idea what it's like growing up with no daddy? How could he learn to be a man? He didn't know how to act or what to say. He never learned sports, and probably learned about sex at the school playground. He never asked me about it. If he'd asked you, you'd probably tell him he was supposed to like *boys* instead of girls, just to torment him."

"Look, I'm not going to apologize for stupid things I did as a kid."

"Oh, I blame you for lots of things with my Craig," she went on, "but I shoulder my own blame as well. I always used you as an example, and maybe that wasn't so smart of me. But what's done is done. It makes no difference now." She tossed her gloves to the ground. "Tell me what you want and then go away so I don't have to look at you anymore."

"Mary, I never meant for things to be like this. You have to believe—"

"Tell me before I change my mind."

He sighed. "Did Craig ever mention a book called *Perdum?*"

She laughed—a dark, humorless sound. "Did you come to this town for the sole purpose of tormenting me? Is that what you're trying to do?"

"I'm not trying to do anything. All I want to know—"

"I know about the book. It was something that belonged to his daddy. He treasured it and carried it everywhere."

"Do you know where it is?"

Mary's lower lip began to tremble. "If you would have cared enough to come to the funeral, you would have known."

Andy's breath stopped. "Why?"

She said, "It was the one thing he wanted to be buried with, and I put it in the casket myself."

42

Kate sat motionless on the couch, staring at the small white box in her hands. The woman on the front looked like she had just won the lottery: both hands were pressed to her cheeks and her mouth was a giant circle. Kate wasn't sure why she had bought the damn thing, because there was no way she was pregnant, *especially* by three weeks. Surely there would be other symptoms, other signs. She had felt fine before coming to Mortom. *Fine.* She was a fool for thinking otherwise.

The front door opened, and she crammed the pregnancy test in her pocket as Andy came up the staircase.

"It returns," she said. "How lucky for me."

His face was expressionless as he sat at the table, and she crossed her arms in anticipation of what was coming next. Whatever it was, she had no doubt it was going to be glorious.

"I tracked down my book," he said. "The one I needed for the next clue."

"Wonderful. So what are you off to do next? Ransack the basement? Tear up the closets? Please, don't keep me in suspense."

He didn't speak. His eyes were fastened on the floor.

"So what's the next move?" she asked.

He cleared his throat. "Leaving."

"Leaving," she repeated. "And what exactly does that mean?"

"It means going back home. Today."

An incredulous laugh escaped her mouth. "After all the shit you've put us through, you expect me to believe that?"

"I'm serious, Kate. Just hear me out."

There was something in his tone that made her pause—a heaviness, almost—but she still didn't trust him. She would give him just enough rope to hang himself.

"Fine," she said stiffly. "Talk."

"A lot . . . happened today. So much, in fact, that it made me realize a few things. As obvious as it sounds, I realized that everything comes at a cost, and sometimes that cost is high. Maybe even too high . . ."

He leaned back and shook his head.

"I should have never involved you in any of this. I've made a mess of things here, and as of right now I'm taking full responsibility for my actions. It's my job to clean it up, not yours, and that's what I need to do."

"Wait a minute," she said. "I thought you just said we were leaving."

"Not *we*, Kate. You."

"Me?"

"You're going to drive the truck back to Luther. In a few days I'll catch a bus in Keota and come home."

"No," she said, shaking her head. "No . . . I don't think that's a good idea at all."

"Yes, it is. I've given this a lot of thought, and it's for the best. I'll spend a couple days going through the house and getting things in order. I'd also like to make peace with Mary, if that's possible at this point. Once all that is done, I'll be able to leave and put this place behind me."

He set the keys on the table. She stared at them, already replaying the conversation in her head.

"Andy, what are you not telling me?"

"Look, I just . . . You just need to go, okay? I don't want to involve you anymore."

"And I'm not stepping one foot outside this house until you level with me. What aren't you telling me?"

He met her eyes. "None of this is your concern anymore. Don't make a big deal out of it."

"A big deal? You're obviously trying to get rid of me. I'd say this is a *very* big deal."

"It's decided. End of discussion. You can go on your own, or—"

"Or what?" she asked sharply. "You'll call the police and have me removed from the property? Is this really how warped your mind has become? That you can't trust anyone anymore, not even me? Just because Carol—"

"Don't," he said, pointing a finger at her.

"Andy, what she did to you . . . You have to move past it. It wasn't your fault. You can't just give up on everything because things didn't work out."

"Leave it alone, Kate," he said through clenched teeth as he stood. "I'm warning you."

"Why can't you see I'm trying to help—"

"I don't want or need your help!" he nearly screamed. "Can't you get it through your head that I don't want you here anymore?"

He knocked over his chair and stormed down the staircase.

"Don't do this!" she called after him. "You can't keep pushing everyone away!"

She went to the top of the staircase. She could hear him in the basement, moving things around.

"I won't leave you," she said. Her voice began to warble and she realized she was on the verge of tears. "Andy . . . you can trust me. You just have to let me in. Let me in and I can help you. I know I can."

She straightened up as he reappeared in the foyer holding her suitcase.

"Hey," she said. "What—"

It was all she got out before he opened the door and flung her suitcase into the yard.

"What are you doing?" she shrieked.

She ran down and pushed past him. The moment she was outside he closed the door.

"Hey!"

She tried the knob. It didn't turn.

"Andy!" she shouted, pounding on the door. "Unlock this!"

His face appeared in the glass. "Look down."

"What?"

He jabbed his finger downward. She took a step back and saw the pickup keys. She snatched them up with a snarl.

"This isn't funny—" she began.

He was gone.

She stared at the door, unable to believe what had just happened. Of all the assholes she had dated in her life (more than she liked to admit), she had never *once* been tossed onto the street. It had taken her brother to accomplish that feat of infamy.

"Fine," she said.

If that was how he wanted to play it, then so be it. She was done beating herself up, done trying to help. He could hide in the house and rot for all she cared.

She carried her suitcase to the pickup and climbed inside. Her mouth began to tremble as she slid the key into the ignition.

"No," she said fiercely. Her fingers tightened around the wheel, hard enough to drain her knuckles white. "You're not going to get upset. Not anymore."

She backed into the street. Her eyes fell on the Simms house, and a knot twisted her stomach. She had completely forgotten about Debbie, the one person in this town that actually did want her around.

She pulled the pickup to the curb and took a pen and paper from her bag. She wrote with a shaky hand, quickly at first and then with more difficulty.

Debbie,

I have decided to head back home. I'm sorry we didn't get more time together, but I want you to know I think you are an amazing young woman, and I'm grateful I had the opportunity to get to know you. Always remember that life can be messy and complicated at times, but in the end, everything always works out for the best.

—Kate

She walked the note to the door and left it sticking halfway out, knowing Ricky would probably find it first and tear it to shreds. It was the best she could do.

She returned to the pickup and sped off without looking back, wanting to put distance between her and Mortom as quickly as possible.

43

Three o'clock.

Jack Thatcher sits in his office, thinking about Andy Crowl. Twice
he has seen the man's truck in Craig's driveway, and his patience is
running out. Mortom is a nice, small town, and it doesn't need people
like him around.

A few minutes before four, Nate Shawler puts down his crossword
and wonders if Andy is doing okay. Their last conversation was some-
what strained, and he hopes nothing more has transpired between
Andy and Ricky Simms. Nate would never forgive himself if something bad happened to Andy, especially because of what he told him.

Four fifteen finds Mary Moore sitting at her kitchen table, holding a worn photograph in her trembling hand. Craig is sitting atop a
plastic giraffe at the Keota zoo, his mouth drawn into a laugh, his eyes
wide and excited. The color in the picture is faded and dull: a snapshot
in time. It is forever gone, like Craig, and all that remains are the lies
that tore them apart.

Five o'clock. Ricky Simms stirs his soup, but mostly he thinks of
the people across the street. Debbie is still talking to that woman behind

his back, and more than once he has caught the man stealing glances in Debbie's direction. If things continue this way, things are going to end badly for everyone involved. No one makes a fool of Ricky Simms twice. No one.

Five thirty finds Debbie Simms lying on her bed, staring at the ceiling. In her hand is Kate's note. Kate has abandoned her, just like her parents and Craig and everyone else. All she wants to do is go somewhere where no one knows her; then she can never be hurt again.

Six o'clock. Andy makes his way downtown to the hardware store. There is a specific item he requires—one Craig does not seem to own.

The clerk greets him warmly at the door, even though the store has closed five minutes prior. Andy is directed to the back of the store and finds what he needs. The clerk makes small talk as he rings up the transaction, and Andy smiles and nods and pays with cash.

On the walk back he is friendly to everyone he passes. It is a beautiful day and soon everything will be set right. It is only a matter of time now.

Back at the house he places the shovel inside the door and sits on the couch. There is no angst or anxiety within him, only calm. He is content to sit and wait. There is much to be done, but not until dark.

He checks his watch.

He waits.

44

Andy stood at the foot of the grave, unmoving and unblinking. The cigarette between his fingers burned forgotten as he stared at the dirt, trying to feel something for the man buried below. Not just any man: his own flesh and blood. A week ago Craig had been walking around the town of Mortom, breathing air and living life. And in the blink of an eye, he was gone. When his mother had called and told Andy the news, he felt nothing. When Thatcher left a message about the estate, he returned the call immediately. He had skipped the funeral and come for the stuff . . . but there was no stuff, only a rat under a fridge. A dead rat with a key shoved inside its dead mouth. And with that, the game. And there he stood, about to do the unthinkable for something he wasn't sure even existed. Nothing had ever felt so wrong to him in his life.

A car drove past and he watched the taillights disappear into the horizon. The gravesite sat far enough back that the highway wasn't a concern, but if a car drove right up into the cemetery . . . well, then things would get interesting. The temptation to wait until later that night was strong, but moving dirt was going to be a timely chore, and he maybe—*maybe*—had six hours until sunup. He wasn't sure it was even possible for one man with one shovel to move six feet in six hours. The hole he had dug at the shed had knocked the wind out of him, and that was nothing compared to what he was about to do.

He pitched his cigarette and ran a sweaty hand across his forehead. If he was going to do this, it was time to get moving. No more stalling.

He picked up the shovel. It felt impossibly heavy in his hands, and he told himself again how simple it would be to walk away. He could go back to the house, have a few beers, and blissfully pass out on the couch. In the morning he would catch a bus back to Luther and put all this behind him.

"Let sleeping dogs lie," he whispered.

How many times had their mother uttered those words? Hundreds? Thousands? Never had the phrase felt more apt. And he truly believed what he had told Kate earlier: some things were meant to stay buried. He believed that. He did.

But some things had to be discovered.

Craig hadn't been insane. Not in the traditional sense, anyway. There was entirely too much method in this madness, and that meant Craig had been driven by another force, one as equally powerful, destructive, and unpredictable. Mary could talk until she was blue in the face about how awful he had treated Craig while growing up, but no amount of childhood teasing could drive a man to this level of hate. There was more to the story, more buried below the surface.

And that was why he couldn't walk away.

There was tomorrow to think about. And the next day. And the day after. He would spend every day of the rest of his life wondering what it all meant, never knowing the full truth. Never understanding why it had come to this.

And that was unacceptable.

So there he stood. The alternative was simple. Dig six feet into the ground, break open the coffin, and pry the book from Craig's rotting fingers. If that was what needed to be done, then that was what he was going to do. Right or wrong. End of story.

"No choice," he said.

He raised the shovel.

45

Kate tried the doorknob and wasn't surprised to find it locked; it was well past midnight and Andy had probably passed out on the couch. That was her hope, anyway. Catching him half-asleep was her best bet in talking sense into him. If that didn't work, she wasn't sure what she would do. All she knew was she didn't have it in her to drive another two hours toward home before turning back around. Four hours of road, radio, and tears had emotionally drained her. It had also given her time to think, and the bottom line was that you didn't abandon family. Ever. She would get through to him, no matter what it took. Assuming, of course, she could get back inside the house.

She circled into the backyard and tried the patio door. It was also locked. That left two options. Repeatedly ring the bell to wake him (and undoubtedly piss him off to a greater degree), or wait until morning. Both choices sucked. Mary probably had a spare key, but it wasn't as though Kate could stroll over and ask for it at this hour. And without a key, there was no other way inside.

"Unless," she said, remembering how Mary had come through the garage and scared her to death. That meant there had to be a door that opened into the garage.

She found it on the side of the house, partially hidden behind a large bush . . . and also partially ajar. The light above the workbench was lit, and the door that led into the basement stood half-open as well. This wasn't like Andy at all, especially after everything that had happened.

She took a step back, unsure how to proceed, and felt an immediate wave of relief when Craig's bedroom light popped on. Everything fell into place: Andy had left to go somewhere, forgotten the key, and come back in through the garage. She had probably just missed him by a matter of minutes.

She maneuvered her way through the sea of cans in the garage and locked the basement door behind her.

"Andy?" she hollered up the stairs. "Don't freak out; it's only me!"

No answer. He was either out of earshot or serving up the silent treatment.

She took the staircase and gave a weary smile when she saw Craig's door was shut and the light was now off. Did he really think she was just going to go away if he pretended to be asleep?

She went to the door. "Don't be mad, okay? I was halfway home and I couldn't do it. I couldn't leave you here alone."

She placed her hand on the knob.

"Can I please come in and talk to you? I know you're awake; I saw the light on from outside." She smiled and added in a playful voice, "If you're pretending to be asleep like you did when we were kids, it's not going to work."

She waited a moment longer and turned the knob. The door swung open, casting a long shadow from the hallway inside the bedroom.

"Andy?"

Her fingers brushed the inside wall in search of the light switch . . . and when a hand grabbed her wrist, she began to scream.

THURSDAY

46

3:37 p.m.

A phone was ringing.

Andy lifted his head and tried to open his eyes. The sun through the window was blinding, and he rolled to one side, knocking over a half dozen beer bottles. Exactly *why* there were beer bottles in his bed he didn't want to know, and it wasn't until he managed to keep his lids open for more than a second that he realized he was lying on the living room floor, fully dressed and wearing his shoes.

He sat up and winced; everything above his neck felt like it was caught in a vise grip. He tried to remember how much he had drunk and quickly decided he didn't want to know.

The phone cut out as he staggered into the kitchen and picked up the aspirin on the counter. He shook three in his hand, considered, and added three more. He was going to need it to get through the next few hours. Today was about one thing and one thing alone: getting the hell out of Mortom. Which was easier said than done. The first obstacle was getting to Keota. A cab ride (assuming he could even *get* a cab to come this far) would probably cost a small fortune. There was a chance Nate might be willing to drive him, but that was a pretty big thing to ask of a relationship that was primarily based on the exchange of money and goods. Worst-case scenario was he would ask Mary to drive him. She'd probably be thrilled to get him out of town. *Absolute* worst-case scenario he would hitchhike. Twenty miles wasn't a walk in the park, but it was hardly impossible. Once he was in Keota he would find a bus terminal and be on his way back home, ready to start over and live out a long, boring, uneventful life. He thought that sounded just fine.

The phone began to ring again. It was probably Kate, calling to read him the riot act. And if he didn't pick up, she would probably keep calling, and there was no way he could handle listening to that noise for the next hour.

He grabbed the phone. "What?"

"Mr. Crowl? This is Jack Thatcher."

"*Shit*," Andy hissed as he caught sight of the clock and saw it was after three. He had slept away most of the day.

"Excuse me?"

"Nothing. What do you want?"

"I have told you multiple times that it's highly inappropriate for you to be inside the house, even for a brief amount of time. When I contacted Mary in search of you, she said you've been staying there—"

"Don't get your panties in a twist. I'm tired and frustrated and done with this town and all the people in it. So you don't have to worry about me anymore, because as soon as I hang up this phone I'm outta here. Go ahead and sell the house, pocket your percentage, and mail me a check if there's anything left. I'll stop by the bank on my way out of town to sign whatever else needs to be signed, but until then don't bother me again."

He slammed down the phone and cringed at the sound. The day was already shaping into crap and he hadn't been awake for five minutes.

There was a knock on the front door and he let out a groan. This was all he needed right now. With his luck it was Mary, coming to hurl more insults at him about what a horrible human being he was. Or better yet, maybe it was Ricky Simms. Maybe he had somehow found out about his adventure at the cemetery last night and was coming over to confront him. Let him come. Craig's precious grave hadn't been touched, so unless being in the cemetery with a shovel was a crime in itself, Ricky had nothing on him.

He started down the staircase. The front door was halfway open (how drunk *had* he been?), and he saw Debbie standing on the porch, holding a piece of paper. He could only imagine what mess he was about to step into now.

"Hey," he said cautiously. "This really isn't the best time—"

"Is she really gone?" Debbie asked.

"Gone," Andy said, trying to sort his thoughts. "Kate. Um, yeah . . . she took off last night in my truck."

"She left me this note."

Debbie held up the paper. He gave it an indifferent glance before looking past her at the street. "Hey, I don't think your grandfather would be very happy if he saw you standing here, so . . . you know . . ."

"Sure, okay."

She pulled on the screen door and started to come inside.

"Whoa," Andy said, blocking her. "That's not exactly what I meant."

"She never said good-bye," Debbie said. "She told me we were friends and I could trust her, but then she left me."

Andy half shrugged. "Something came up. Don't take it personally, okay?"

"It's a pretty crappy thing to do. Why would she do that to me?"

She stared at him, as if waiting for him to somehow make things right. It was also apparent she had no intention of simply turning around and leaving.

"I'll tell her to call you, okay?"

"Grandpa wouldn't let me talk to her."

"Ah. Well, um . . . how about this? I'll give you her phone number, and then *you* can call her when your grandpa's not around. Sound good?"

"He'd see the charge on the long distance bill."

She was still watching him. He pushed out a long sigh, knowing he was going to regret this but also knowing it was probably the quickest way to get this resolved.

"Did you want to call her now?" he asked heavily. "I guess you can use the phone in the kitchen if you *really* want to."

Her face lit up. "That'd be awesome. Yeah."

He moved aside and checked the street before following her up, already regretting the decision.

"Be quick, okay?" He punched out the number and passed over the phone. "And let yourself out when you're done."

He went onto the deck. The last thing he needed was to get involved with one of Kate's causes; he had enough of his own problems to deal with. He needed to have his head examined for letting Debbie inside.

"There was no answer," Debbie said, sitting in one of the patio chairs.

"Uh, your grandfather—"

"He mows the new cemetery on Thursdays. It takes him most of the day." Her eyes drifted around the deck. "I used to sit out here with Craig. He'd always have lemonade for me. Sometimes he'd say things about you."

Andy's heart skipped a beat. "What kinds of things?"

"He told me about the summer he stayed with you when he was twelve. Best summer of his life, he said. You had a tree fort and the two of you were explorers. He even showed me the rock."

"The rock?"

"The smooth one that looks like a bird's egg. He said you both found it in the woods and you told him he should keep it. I'm surprised you didn't find it inside the house. It's sitting on his desk. I can show you where it is if you want to have it back. The pencil holder is also there."

Andy was almost afraid to ask. "Pencil holder?"

"The clay one you made for Craig. He said it was a Christmas gift."

Andy felt his insides shift. His mother had forced him to get Craig a gift that year, and the pencil holder was something he had found at the bottom of his closet.

"But sometimes," Debbie said in a hushed voice, "he would get weird."

"Weird like how?"

"Sometimes after he'd tell a story about you, he'd get *really* quiet. He'd sit there and stare out into space, and you couldn't tell if he was sad or mad. It was almost like he was somewhere else inside his head, thinking real hard about things."

"Did Craig . . ." He hesitated, trying to choose his words carefully. "Did he seem . . . *angry* with me before his death? Did he talk about me a lot then?"

Debbie looked away. "I didn't see him very much right before he died. My grandpa . . . They weren't talking, and I wasn't supposed to see him. The last time I saw him was at the funeral."

The last part came out as no more than a whisper.

"Grandpa doesn't know that," she added. "He was at work and I snuck out and went there. I didn't go inside, though. Not with the people there. If I did that, he might have found out. I just stood by the window and watched. But when everybody left . . ."

Andy leaned forward. "What?"

Debbie swallowed. "I saw the funeral guy close the lid on the coffin. Then he left the room and no one was inside. So I went in. I had to say good-bye. I wanted to see him one last time, so I lifted the lid . . . I looked inside . . ."

Tears filled her eyes. Andy had an idea of was what coming next.

"I saw him," she said softly. "Grandpa said that sometimes when people drown it can change how they look . . . but it still looked like Craig . . . but at the same time it didn't. He had on makeup and was dressed in a suit. And there was a book in his hands."

"Book?" Andy felt his breath crawl to a stop. "You saw a book?"

She said, "Every night after supper I would come over and we would read a chapter. It was sort of like *our* book. And it seemed wrong that he was taking it with him. It was the only thing I could remember him by. And I wanted . . . I wanted . . ."

"What?" he asked in a strained voice. He was pitched forward, his face a perfect shade of white. "You wanted to *what*?"

"I took it!" she cried. "I took it and closed the coffin and ran out! But I didn't mean to! I swear!"

She let out a sob and buried her face in her hands. All his energy drained to his feet. This whole time the book had been with Debbie, not inside the coffin. And he had come so close to digging . . . The shovel had been raised above the dirt . . .

"I'm sorry," Debbie moaned. "I'm *so* sorry. I knew it was wrong, and I really didn't even realize what I'd done until it was too late, and then all I wanted to do was put it back, but I couldn't."

"You still have it?" His mouth was cotton dry.

She swiped at her cheek with her sleeve. "Yeah . . ."

"Where is it?"

"I didn't mean to take it," Debbie said again. "Please don't tell any-one. You won't, will you?"

"No, I won't tell." His heart was jackhammering inside his chest and it was a struggle to keep his voice neutral. "And nobody's going to be mad at you, okay? You know that, right?"

She nodded, but hesitantly.

"Debbie, where is the book now?"

She sniffled. "Under my bed. I hid it so Grandpa wouldn't see it."

"Did you know the book is special for me, too? It's something I've been searching for."

Her face began to twitch and pull. "And you couldn't find it because I took it—"

"No," he said, shaking his head. "This is a *good* thing. If not for you, the book would have been gone forever. You saved it."

She stared at him dubiously.

"And you know what else? I think Craig would have wanted you to have it. So it's fine . . . No, it's *perfect* that you took it. I mean that."

"For real?"

"Yeah," he answered. "For *real*. And it would mean a lot to me if I could see it. Do you think I could take a look at it?"

"I guess . . ."

"Right now," he said. "You can go get it right now and bring it to me?"

She drew back slightly and he told himself to take it down a notch. His hands were shaking so badly he had them locked together behind his back.

"I'm sorry," he said. "It's just . . . it's kind of important I see the book as soon as I can. It would mean so much to me. And Kate. It would mean a lot to her also."

"I can get it," she said quietly. "I'll go now."

"I really appreciate this. And so does Kate. And, hey . . . while you're getting it, I'll try calling her again. She's probably asleep, but I'll keep ringing until she hears it and wakes up."

He followed her through the kitchen and picked up the phone as she went down the staircase.

"I'm trying right now," he told her, "so don't be too long. I'll keep her on the phone until you get back, okay?"

Debbie looked over her shoulder as she went out the door. As soon as she was out of sight Andy hung up the phone and moved to the other side of the kitchen. Through the front window he could see her walking up to her house. In a few seconds she would come back with the book and everything would be back on track.

There was absolutely nothing to worry about.

47

Five minutes later Andy was pressed against the window in a near panic, still waiting for Debbie to reemerge. A thousand thoughts raced through his head, each worse than the last: she had misplaced the book; her grandfather had found it and thrown it out; she had made the whole thing up and wasn't coming back. The girl had already proven herself a liar . . . Who was to say this wasn't another plea for attention?

He straightened up as she came out of the house. There was a plastic grocery bag in her hands, and he was down the staircase in a matter of seconds. He held open the door as she crossed the lawn and came up the steps.

"Here," she said.

He took the bag with an unsteady hand. Through the plastic he could see the word "PERDUM" printed on the cover in big, gold letters.

"I'll take good care of it," he promised.

"I don't want it back. It doesn't feel right to keep it."

"Sure," he said, barely hearing her words. He slid the book from the bag. The dust jacket was worn and faded but otherwise looked normal. Nothing was sticking out from the pages.

"Did you get a hold of Kate?" Debbie asked.

"Huh?" He raised his head with a frown. "Oh. Um, no . . . she didn't answer. But I'll keep trying."

"If Grandpa goes out later, can I stop back and check again?"

"Sure," he said absently. He started up the staircase without taking his eyes from the book. "Yeah . . . do that."

He carried the book to the dining room and sat at the table. This was it, the moment of truth. Everything he had done, all he had gone through . . . it all pointed to this.

And that scared the living shit out of him.

He wasn't supposed to have this book. No one in their right mind would dig up a body, and Craig would have known this. If not for luck and chance, this book would not be sitting in front of him. All he could do now was pray that Craig had followed through and kept his word.

Andy opened the cover. Writing was scribbled in the corner of the first page:

Craig—
This book belonged to your daddy
and I know he would have wanted
you to have it.
—Mom

He turned the page and saw "Perdum" with the author's name underneath. The next page had copyright information, and the following page started the first chapter. There was nothing out of the ordinary.

He moved to the next page. More printed words. No bookmarks, no secret messages.

"Something will be here," he assured himself.

The next page had a small tear in the corner but was otherwise normal.

He moved on, a little quicker now. The book was massive; it was going to take forever to get through it—

His breath came to a dead stop when he saw the word *forty* half-way down the page. It had been highlighted with an orange marker.

"Son of a bitch," he whispered.

When he got up to find something to write with, his legs were shaking so badly he could hardly walk.

48

4:11 p.m.

He was almost to the end of the book when he came across the word *rattle*. He started to add it to the list and stopped when he realized only half the word was highlighted. Or to be more exact, the first three letters.

"Rat," he whispered.

He picked up his notepad and scanned through the words he had written. The fifth word was *food*.

Rat food.

He stared at the words, turning them over in his head. The rat had started the game and the cage was still downstairs . . . but he didn't remember seeing any food. What would rat food have to do with anything?

He shifted uneasily and thought again of Kate telling him it was all a joke with a big "ha-ha" waiting at the end. But there was no way. He couldn't, *wouldn't* believe that.

He added *rat* to the list and pulled the book closer. The highlighter seemed to be growing fainter with each new word he found, and twice he had gone back to make sure he hadn't missed anything. It was going to be difficult enough putting the words in order as it was, but working with an incomplete list would make it damn near impossible.

"*One*," he read aloud. Bottom of the page, last word in the paragraph. He wrote it next to the word *rat*. Eleven words total now.

His fingers worked the pages as his eyes moved back and forth. New chapter . . . nothing highlighted. Next page . . . nothing. Next page, middle paragraph: *left*. He jotted it down.

He turned the page. *Hope* was highlighted in the first sentence. He put it on the pad. There were maybe ten pages left. He maneuvered them carefully, sometimes scanning each page twice, watching for anything else.

It was on the second-to-last page he saw it: two commas with a dot of highlight over each of them. The marks were so small it was a miracle he noticed them at all. He added them to the list and turned to the last page. There was nothing else. He closed the book and let out a shaky breath. It was done.

still	forty	you	only
food	east	have	miles
go	rat	one	left
hope	,	,	

Thirteen words and two commas, somehow all fitting together. This wasn't a puzzle like the others—this was information. Information that was going to lead him to the end.

"Okay," he whispered. "I got this."

He ran his eyes over the words, rearranging them in his head and trying to establish the obvious. *Rat* and *food*. Too coincidental to disregard. He wrote it at the bottom of the page and crossed those two words off the list.

"Forty miles . . . east . . . *Go* forty miles east . . ."

The tip of the pencil hovered over the pad as his mind put it together and took it apart, over and over again. It was almost *too* obvious. Then again, if he was convinced the riddle was going to direct him to a physical location, then driving forty miles east fit that theory perfectly . . .

He wrote down the sentence and crossed off the words. Obvious or not, directions didn't get much clearer than that. Maybe the directions would take him to a pet store that sold rat food. And from there it would be a simple matter of digging a hole in the middle of the store. Or searching all the items on the shelves for something hidden. Or killing the store clerk who swallowed the next key because Craig paid him to—

"Keep it together," he warned himself.

His eyes traced the remaining words, putting them together, creating and rejecting.

"Hope . . . you . . . only still . . . have one . . . left . . ."

He tapped at the commas with the pencil. Since there were two, it was logical to assume there were three sentences. The challenge was figuring out where the sentences stopped and began.

"You only have one . . . left . . . still . . ."

His eyes jumped back and forth between *rat food* and *forty miles*. Those were the only two things he was almost positive fit together, so that was where he needed to build from. The other words in the list were so vague they could fit almost anywhere.

"Rat food," he said. "Left rat food . . . still rat food . . . one rat food . . . have rat food . . ."

He blindly reached for his cigarettes and cursed when he remembered they were gone.

"Have rat food . . ."

He wrote it on the pad and studied it. Almost without thinking he added the word *still* before it.

"Still have rat food," he read.

It was almost a question, but there weren't question marks to use, only commas. Providing *go forty miles east* was its own sentence.

"Still have rat food," he said again.

He drew a faint pencil line through *still* and *have*. Not a question, unless . . .

He pulled the pad close and examined the remaining five words. He wrote

HOPE YOU STILL HAVE RAT FOOD

His gaze moved to the staircase, trying to remember if he had seen anything in the basement that resembled pet food. It would probably be in a bag, tucked away on a shelf or pushed under the stairs. Maybe even hidden in a corner, just out of sight. And if it was there and he did find it, something would be inside. And maybe that something would have something to do with something forty miles away. And once he found that other something, then something else would something—

"Dammit!"

He flung the pencil across the room and pushed away from the table. Craig was messing with him, mocking him. It didn't make sense because it wasn't supposed to. None of it meant anything.

He went onto the deck. The day was bright and warm, full of life, and he felt none of it. He had completely and utterly cannibalized his mind, body, and spirit. And for what? A little bit of money? Some answers to questions he never asked? Craig's game wasn't about following clues to a goal; it was about seeing how far someone could be pushed. How far they were willing to go. *That* was the goal.

"Rat food," he said with a dark chuckle.

He moved back inside but stopped shy of the table. He could see the notepad from where he stood, and all at once he was furious with himself. There was no way in hell he was going to let two little words be his undoing, not after everything he had already accomplished. He just needed to keep it together for a little while longer. Craig had led him this far, and he had to trust that it would all come together in the end. If he gave up now, Craig would win. And he couldn't live with that.

He leaned over the table and tried to get his thoughts working again. "Work it out," he told himself. "You got this."

Rat food. Looking for a pet store still seemed the most plausible, but it would be stupid not to check the basement first. Craig's rat had been fat and plump, so it obviously had been eating something. Until Craig had decided to use it as a key holder, anyway. Then it was nothing more—

Andy stopped.

The locker key had been inside the mouth of the rat.

"Rat food," he whispered.

He spun around, trying to go two directions at once. It was the key—the goddamn key in the rat's mouth. *That* was the rat food. And what did that have to do with forty miles east? The key opened some sort of locker there. The answer had been in front of him the whole time.

His hand went into his left pocket and found nothing. He frantically dug into the other pocket, horrified he had left the key inside his truck that was now back in Luther with Kate—

The key was there. He had completely dismissed it when he realized the rat was the clue, but now it made perfect sense. Of course the key opened something; why else would Craig have put it there? The game started with the rat, and now it was going to end with the rat.

For the first time in his life, Andy felt a small admiration for his cousin. If nothing else, Craig had been a clever bastard.

But not clever enough.

Andy picked up the notepad. Only three words remained, and they were easy enough to put together to finish the last sentence.

"Only one left," he read.

49

4:59 p.m.

If the station wagon outside Craig's driveway had been operational, it had been in another lifetime. The moped, on the other hand, had been Craig's primary source of transportation, so it had to run. Andy had barely given it a thought the entire time they had been there, but now it was going to save his ass.

"And look at that," Andy said with an involuntary grin.

The key was sticking out of the ignition. If that wasn't a sign his luck was changing, nothing was.

The moped bounced under his weight as he straddled the seat, and all at once an overwhelming sensation of calm washed over him. Things were going to be okay. He was going to get through this.

He moved the key to the "On" position. It wasn't exactly a motor-cycle, but it was close enough to manage.

He clamped the handlebar brake and pushed the ignition button. The starter whined but didn't catch. He waited a moment and tried again.

Nothing.

The ignition was on, the battery was charged . . . What else was there?

"Gas," he groaned. The needle was on empty. So much for his changing luck.

He climbed off and began to push.

50

5:17 p.m.

"Well, now," Nate said with a chuckle. "*That* looks familiar."

Andy rolled the moped to a stop by the pump and humored him with a mirthless smile. "They weigh a helluva lot more than you think they would."

"I reckon. I was just heading inside to fetch a paper. You need anything?"

"Something to drink would be great."

"Can do."

Andy lifted the nozzle from the pump and tried to ignore the trembling that had taken root in his legs. The smart thing would have been to seek out a gas can and take it *to* the moped, but that would have eaten up more time. It was always about time.

"What happened to the truck?" Nate asked, returning with a soda.

"Long story. Hey, what towns are directly east of here?"

"Big or small?"

"Either."

Nate considered. "Let's see . . . there's Egan, Stockton . . . Stuart . . . Crichton . . ."

"Anything right around forty miles?"

"Stuart is right around forty-five, so far as I would wager. It's bigger than Mortom, but still pretty small."

"Is it hard to find from here?"

Nate laughed. "Not if you can find the highway that runs through the middle of town. Stuart is a straight shot all the way."

The pump clicked off. Andy drained half the soda, handed it back to Nate, and replaced the nozzle. He dug a twenty-dollar bill from his pocket. "This enough to cover everything?"

"And some change left over. Be right back."

"Keep it," Andy said, swinging his leg over the moped. He pressed the ignition button, and the engine sputtered to life.

"You're a good man, Nate," he said. "Don't let anyone tell you otherwise."

"Everything okay?" Nate asked.

"No. But it will be soon."

He drove off before Nate could respond.

51

7:21 p.m.

Andy thought he knew what true misery was, but nothing—absolutely *nothing*—came close to the act of driving a moped on a highway.

The fastest the machine would go was thirty miles an hour, and that was only on a stretch of open road. Whenever he broached a hill, the moped would slow to twenty or sometimes fifteen miles an hour. It was no surprise he was passed by every car, but he could have lived without all the honking, shouting, and middle fingers. One bunch had even tried to peg him with a full bottle of water. It was a small miracle he hadn't been run off the road or killed, and when he finally reached Stuart he was worn out and pissed off.

He pulled into the first station he saw, hoping to pick the brain of the clerk inside. With any luck, he would find a Stuart equivalent of Nate. Instead he found three kids that barely looked out of high school. To make matters worse, the clerk had green hair, the kid leaning against the cooler had a blue Mohawk, and the girl sitting on the floor had so many face piercings Andy wasn't entirely sure it *was* a girl.

"Good evening, good sir," the clerk said. "How may we be of assistance? Gasoline for your chariot?"

The girl snickered.

"I'm good," Andy said. He nodded at the kid with the Mohawk. "You look like a smart guy. Maybe you can help me."

"Uh . . . help you with what?"

"This key." Andy held it up so they could see. "I'm positive it opens a locker in this town. I need some suggestions where to look."

Blank stares all around.

"Bus depot," Andy said loudly, meeting each of their eyes. "Bowling alleys, gyms, train stations . . . Anything like that around here? Anyone?"

"How can you not know what it opens?" the girl asked. "I mean, where did you get it?"

"Maybe his old lady kicked him out," the clerk said. "And then, maybe she hid his stuff and mailed him the key. That would suck."

"Yeah," Andy said. "That would suck."

"It could be for a hotel," Mohawk said.

"Dumb ass," said the girl. "Why would a hotel have lockers? Let me see it."

Andy hesitated for a moment before passing it over. His eyes stayed on it as the girl turned it over in her hands.

"Is there a reward for helping?" the clerk asked.

"Yeah," said Mohawk. "Like, if you find a treasure, we should get some of it."

"Try the rec center," the girl said, handing it back. "And ignore these morons. They mostly talk to hear their own voices."

"Rec center?" Andy asked.

"The recreation center. It's over on Dubuque Street. I hung out there a lot last summer when my boyfriend worked there. That's the only place I can think of that has lockers."

"Can you tell me how to get there?"

She pointed out the glass. "Get back on the road you were on. Follow that until you can't go any farther and then go left. Two streets down, go right. From there it's only a couple blocks. It's a big, ugly building. You can't miss it."

"Thanks."

He went out the door and mounted the moped, replaying the directions in his head. It was as good a place to start as any.

"Hey." The girl was standing in the doorway. "Can I ask you something?"

"What?"

"This has something to do with a girl, doesn't it? You're caught up in some sort of romantic scavenger hunt or something, aren't you?"

He thought of Carol. If she hadn't left, would he be here doing this? She had always been the levelheaded one. She would have talked him out of it.

"Isn't it always about a girl?" he asked.

She smiled. If not for all the face junk, she might have been pretty.

"I hope you find what you're looking for," she said.

He started the moped with a grimace. "I have to. It's all I've got left."

He sputtered off without looking back.

52

7:52 p.m.

The girl had been right about one thing: The rec center couldn't be missed. It sat smack in the center of town, was easily a hundred years older than any of the buildings around it, and most of its brick had been marred with incoherent graffiti. The girl's directions, on the other hand, had been shit, and it had taken another stop at a different gas station—this one helmed by a very friendly and knowledgeable lady— for him to find the place. It already felt like too much trouble for what undoubtedly was going to be another dead end.

A bell went off over his head as he stepped through the door, and the man behind the desk lowered his newspaper just enough to peer over it. "Help ya?"

"So here's the deal," Andy said with a big smile. "The wife thinks we need to start exercising, and she asked me to come down and check out the facilities. I was hoping I could wander around a bit."

The man raised the paper. "Knock yourself out."

"You have a pool, right? Boy, the wife sure likes to swim."

"End of the hall." The newspaper opened and closed. "Hours and prices are posted by the community bulletin board next to the drinking fountain."

"Thanks."

He wandered to the board and gave it a quick glance. The fliers tacked across it were so dense it was hard to tell where one ended and another began. Apartments for rent, cars for sale . . . auditions for a school production . . .

"School," he said, unaware he was speaking the words aloud. "Schools have lockers in the hallways."

"Something wrong, pal?"

Andy quickly summoned a smile. "Sorry. I, uh . . . just thought of something."

The man gave him a once-over with his eyes. "We close at eight."

"Got it. I'll be quick."

He pulled down the flier and stared at it as he started toward the pool. A locker inside a school had never crossed his mind . . . but was that really plausible? Schools didn't exactly let people wander the halls, and someone like Craig would have stuck out like a sore thumb. So how exactly did he think Craig not only got inside, but also managed to hide something inside a student's locker? And while he was on the subject, didn't school lockers use combination locks, not keys?

"Yep," he told himself with a bitter smile. "And you're an idiot."

He crumpled the flier in his hand, pushed open the locker room door . . . and found himself standing in front of a row of green lockers.

For a long time he didn't move. He told himself this was nothing more than coincidence, and he wasn't going to get his hopes up. There was no way this was it.

He brought out the key. It matched the heads of the others. He told himself most locker keys looked the same. It didn't mean anything. It was crazy to think it meant anything. He would go to the locker, try the key, and when nothing happened he would *calmly* turn around, walk back out, and continue to search the town. No harm, no foul.

"Twenty-three," he whispered.

It was two lockers down. He went to it, guided the key to the lock, and felt a catch in his throat as the tumblers fell into place.

The locker door swung open. Inside was a single item. It wasn't cash or jewels . . . It wasn't treasure of any kind. Of all the things he could have found, he hadn't expected this.

The videotape had no labels or stickers. It was rewound to the beginning and looked new in its package. Even the recording tab was intact.

He lifted it out, feeling uneasy. No, he hadn't expected this at all. This was supposed to be *it*, the final reward. Not something to lead him somewhere else.

"Unless . . ."

Maybe the videotape was going to tell him where to go to *find* the prize. It wasn't another clue; it was the final information. "Go ten steps from wooden fence and dig under giant rock . . ." Something along those lines. That had to be it. With a little luck it would be near the house and easily accessible. Hell, for all he knew it was buried in the backyard. That would be a fitting final irony: the whole time the prize had been less than twenty feet from where he was staying. The thought made him want to laugh and scream at the same time.

His eyes drifted to the wall clock. It was almost eight, and he told himself to keep moving. The last thing he needed was the guy at the front desk to walk in on him. He could only imagine trying to explain the videotape in his hands.

He tucked the tape under his arm and paused at the doorway. If the guy tried to stop or question him, he would run. It was as simple as that. He would claw and fight his way out the door if he had to.

He opened the door and hurried down the hallway. The guy was nowhere in sight, and Andy's fingers tightened around the tape as he crossed the lobby. A moment later he was out the door, standing on the sidewalk and taking in the cool night air. He was so close to the end he could almost taste it.

He swung a leg over the moped and looked at the tape. There was no way to secure it inside the milk crate, and trying to hold it the entire drive back was only asking for trouble.

"Hell," he muttered.

He sank it down the front of his pants and shifted uncomfortably. If nothing else, it would keep him awake.

He kicked the moped to life and thought of Kate. He was sorry she had gone. If she hadn't left, he would have his truck and wouldn't be stuck on a stupid motorized bicycle.

He checked his mirrors, took in a breath, and sputtered off into the fading light.

53

.

Andy coasted into Mortom with a single disturbing thought running through his head: What if the tape led him to the prize and the prize was somewhere in Stuart? If he had been thinking clearly, he would have found a hotel and watched it there. That would have given him time to rest and plan his next move. Now there was a chance he was going to have to head back to the town he had just left. Of course, this was all assuming Craig had a videotape player. He didn't remember seeing one in the living room, but it wasn't the type of thing a person noticed unless they were looking for it. He also made a mental note to carefully inspect the player before inserting the tape. Craig had probably taken the extra step of pouring syrup or something inside, just to keep things interesting. At this point, nothing was going to surprise him . . . nothing except seeing his truck sitting in the driveway.

He parked next to it with a scowl. He should have expected this. Had he really thought Kate was just going to go and leave him be? That would have been too easy. He was impressed she had stayed away as long as she had before returning. Not that it changed anything. Nothing—and no one—was going to get in his way now.

He took the porch steps in a jog. The house was dark with the shades drawn, and he could all too well visualize Kate sitting at the table with crossed arms, waiting to jump on him the moment he was inside. He felt a rush of anger at the thought and jerked open the door.

"Kate!"

No answer.

"I know you're here!" he shouted. "I don't appreciate you coming back—"

"She ain't here." The voice was terse, male, and unrecognizable. "You best come up. I ain't gonna sit here all night. Already been here an hour and your sister prolly ain't too happy about that."

That got Andy moving. He bolted up the staircase into darkness and frantically groped the wall for the light switch. The videotape slipped from his fingers, and he spun around, heart pounding.

"Kate!"

His eyes fell on the orange dot hovering in the corner by the window. The man inhaled from the cigarette, briefly illuminating the lower half of his face.

"Kate! Can you hear me?"

"I already told ya, she ain't here. She's all tucked away, safe and sound. We'll talk about her in a minute. Right now we need to talk about you."

"If you hurt her—"

"Blah, blah, blah. You talk pretty tough for someone who don't even know what he's dealin with."

There was a rustling of noise and Andy instinctively raised his hands to his face. Light flooded the room, momentarily blinding him, and it took a moment for his eyes to focus. There was no monster there, not even a man. It was the kid from the gas station: Nate's nephew.

"You," Andy croaked.

"You know what I want," the kid said.

Andy didn't hear; he was sprinting across the living room at the kid, fists ready, rage pushing his every step. The kid moved fast—so fast that Andy didn't realize what had happened until he was lying on the carpet clutching his stomach with both hands.

"That there was Lefty," said the kid, holding up a curled fist. "And he's got a brother, so you better curb that shit right now. You get me?"

Pain immediately filled Andy's chest as he tried to speak. He rolled to his side and let out a strangled cry.

"Listen up," said the kid, "I just came by to tell you it's almost time, so give me what was promised, I'll let your sister go, and we can be done with this shit. Whaddaya say?"

Andy shook his head furiously. "It . . . I . . ."

"Oh, come on now. I didn't do ya that hard. You take a hit like a girl."

"Kate . . ." He struggled to sit upright as the air slowly came back, filling his lungs. "She doesn't . . . know . . . anything . . ."

"Okay, this shit is gettin old. You wanna play games? I got a game, too. Craig said readin this would help get things movin in the right direction."

Just the mention of Craig's name made Andy's blood run cold.

"Carol Alice Crowl," said the kid. He was reading from a sheet of paper in his hand. "Twelve Mayfield Drive. Works at Brus Insurance Agency and drives a white truck with the license plate G-S-I-6-4-2-8."

Andy stared at him, too horrified to speak.

"And your mom . . . shit, she don't even have no car since she retired. She make your daddy drive her everywhere? I wouldn't stand for that shit. Should I read off their Social Security numbers?"

"No," Andy said sickly.

The kid whapped the sheet with the back of his hand. "Got it all right here. Everything on you, your sister, your folks . . . even your grandparents. They have a dog named Sandy. Real cute little guy, it says. That's sweet."

The kid refolded the sheet with a sigh.

"I just want what was promised to me. That's all. If you want to be all technical, then I guess I got no choice in waitin. But I will be back at midnight. And if you don't give it to me, I'm gonna be payin a lot of folks a lot of visitin. You get me? And it ain't gonna be for no social callin."

The kid started toward the staircase.

"Wait," Andy choked.

"Midnight," the kid said over his shoulder. "And I ain't *never* late, so you best be here and be ready."

Andy fought his way to his feet. The kid was already out the front door, and Andy dragged himself to the staircase in time to hear his truck speeding off.

He used the wall to steady himself and frantically tried to wrap his mind around what had just happened. What did Nate's nephew have to do with anything? And why would Craig set up a game for him to play if he was supposed to give away the prize at the end, especially when he still didn't know where the prize was. Or for that matter, *what* the prize was . . .

"The tape," he whispered.

It was on the floor where it had fallen. He snatched it up and felt another wave of relief when he saw the video player atop the television. Never in his life had a piece of machinery looked so grand.

He carried the tape to the player and pushed it inside. It went in halfway and stopped, as if something was blocking it.

"Shit—"

He clawed it back out, all at once remembering his thought on Craig sabotaging the machine. The tape looked intact, and he carefully set it aside.

He thumbed open the flap on the player and felt inside. His fingertips brushed something hard and plastic, and he slowly drew it out. It was a computer floppy disk. "Craig's Stuff" was written on the label in red ink.

All the energy drained to his feet. It was never going to be over; one clue was always going to lead to another.

The disk began to tremble in his hand, and he shook his head violently side to side. Kate was out there, counting on him. If he needed to find a computer, then he would find a computer.

"Think," he scolded himself.

There wasn't a computer in the house; he was certain of that. So what did that leave? Mary? Even if she did have a computer (which he seriously doubted) would he really want her standing there watching? God only knew what was on the disk. No, Mary was out. And if Mary was out, that pretty much left one option.

He went to the kitchen and found the phone book. Nate's listing was there, and he stared at it long and hard. Nate was a business owner. That meant keeping records. Taxes had to be paid, orders had to be placed, supplies had to be tracked and inventoried. Nate *had* to have a computer.

But Nate also had a nephew, and that nephew had just kicked the piss out of him. Did he really think it was a good idea to call Nate? For all he knew they were in on it together—

"Stop!" he shouted.

His voice echoed through the room, giving him a start, and he ran a shaky hand through his hair. Talking aloud was one thing, but shouting at voices in your head was another. That was a whole new level of scary. He had gotten this far by relying on his gut and trusting his instincts, and if he started second-guessing everything at this point then he might as well quit. Yes, Nate was related to the kid, but so what? Andy was related to Craig, and they were little more than adversaries. Right there proved family didn't mean shit.

He picked up the phone and punched out the number. If Nate didn't answer, then he didn't know what he would do. The only other thought was trying to find someplace in Keota like a copy shop, but nothing would be open this late and there wouldn't be enough time to get there and get back.

There was a click and Andy straightened up. "Hello?"

"This is Nate," droned Nate's recorded voice. "Leave your name and number and I will call you back."

Andy reset the line and dialed again. When it began to ring, he crossed the living room, threw open the drapes, and impatiently stared down at the empty street below. The neighborhood was dark except for a single lit room at the far end of the Simms house. That was probably Debbie, watching television or reading, maybe even—

The phone slipped away from his ear. *Sending e-mail* was his unfinished thought . . . because really, wasn't that what all kids were about these days? Electronic gadgets like cell phones and laptops? E-mail was practically a second language to the young. Ricky wouldn't have a computer, but that didn't mean Debbie couldn't have easily brought along a laptop . . . How else would she stay in touch with the world outside Mortom?

"This is Nate," said Nate's voice faintly. "Leave your name and number—"

Andy carried the phone to the kitchen and hung it up. He lingered for a moment, indecisive, then went to the front door. The only other sign of life across the street was the soft glow of television from the living room window. That would be Ricky, sprawled out in a recliner, maybe even asleep. If not, he would be taking a helluva chance. But what other choice did he have? Mary wasn't an option, Nate wasn't answering . . . Debbie was his last hope.

He slipped out the door into the night.

54

10:27 p.m.

Andy squatted beside a shrub across from the lit window, out of breath and cursing himself for more wasted time. Backtracking through all the yards had seemed like a better idea than strolling across the street in plain sight, but after two fences, a clothesline attack, and a shoe full of dog crap, he wasn't so sure, especially if it was all for naught. All he could do now was watch and hope the room belonged to Debbie and not Ricky. He had no doubt Ricky would shoot on sight, especially after what had happened with Craig and Debbie. Or what Ricky *believed* had happened.

A shadow moved past the window, and Debbie came into view, brushing her hair. Now all he had to do was figure out how to get her attention without sending her screaming.

He scurried to the house and positioned himself below the window. It was open—he could hear soft music coming from inside the room— and he told himself he had one chance at this. He took a moment to choose his words before lifting his head toward the window. "Debbie, this is Andy and Kate's in trouble."

He braced himself, waiting for the startled scream.

"Andy?" Her shadow appeared above him, partially blocking the light from the room. "Where are you?"

He rose slowly, careful not to startle her. "Kate's in trouble," he said again. "She needs our help."

"What kind of trouble?"

"Please tell me you have a computer."

For a moment there was such a look of bafflement on her face that Andy almost let loose a hysterical laugh. And why the hell not? He was standing there in the dark, talking through a window to a girl he barely knew, asking if she had a computer. What wasn't completely normal about the situation?

"No," she said, but quickly added, "but I know someone who does."

She picked up the phone and dialed. Andy shifted anxiously, trading glances between the window and street, feeling like the world's biggest pervert. All he needed now was for some late-night jogger to come by and tag him as a voyeur.

"Lester," Debbie said into the phone, "can I come use your computer?" Pause. "Yes, right now. It's really important." She gave Andy a nod. "Good. About five minutes. Thanks."

She came back to the window. "We're set. Wait for me in the backyard."

"Okay."

Andy moved to the back of the house and checked his pocket to make sure the disk was still there. He was going to make it—everything was going to be okay. And when this was over, he was going to send Debbie a giant box of chocolates or flowers or whatever it was teenage girls liked.

Debbie came out through the garage wearing a light jacket and a grave expression. Now she was going to ask what was going on, and for the life of him he had no clue what to tell her. It was too unbelievable and there was no time.

He said, "Your grandfather—"

"Always falls asleep watching the news. Is Kate okay?"

"She will be. I know this is all crazy, but I don't think I can even begin to try to explain."

"This will help Kate, right?"

"Yeah," Andy said. It came out with more conviction than he would have believed he had in him. "This is going to help everybody."

"Then we better get moving."

55

10:46 p.m.

"You didn't say anything about bringing someone," the boy gasped. His eyes bulged behind his glasses as he closed the front door behind him. "If my stepmother wakes up—"

"Lester, your stepmonster is passed out in the den like every night, and who cares about him? He came along because I was afraid to walk over in the dark."

"But who is he?"

"A friend. He's fine."

Lester crossed his arms.

"It's Craig's cousin," she said. "Okay?"

"Boy, *that* figures." He regarded Andy from the corner of his eye. "He doesn't look very friendly."

"We're kind of in a hurry," Andy said.

Lester jerked back like he had been slapped. "Well, I am *so* sorry for slowing you down—"

"Lester!" Debbie hissed.

"But I'm not in the habit of letting strange people into my house in the middle of the night."

"You know what?" Andy said. "You're right. And I don't blame you one bit for being suspicious in this situation. It would be stupid for you *not* to be."

"Exactly," Lester said indignantly.

"And I assure you that if this wasn't of the utmost importance, we would not be putting you in this position. But this is important—*very* important—and I promise you we will be out of here as quick as possible."

"It really is an emergency," Debbie said, touching Lester's shoulder. "Really."

Lester narrowed his eyes. "What do you even need a computer for? My Internet is dial-up and it takes forever for anything to download."

Andy held up the disk. "I need to see what's on this."

"Wow, that thing has to be about a *billion* years old. Nowadays they make things called flash drives that hold about eighty gazillion times more data. You can buy them practically anywhere. Jeez."

"Good to know," Andy said, trying to maintain his tone as his patience slipped another notch. "Can you help us?"

"Uh, yeah," Lester said with a scoffing laugh. "That's kid stuff. It's lucky for you my dad won't buy me a new computer and my old one still has a floppy drive reader. Come on and be quiet."

He led them inside and down the hallway to the last door. Model airplanes filled the room, hanging from the ceiling and sitting on every flat surface possible. Andy bumped one and almost knocked it to the floor.

"*Careful*," Lester seethed, showing off a row of upper braces. "These are fragile."

"Here," Andy said, handing over the disk.

Lester sat at his desk. "There better not be a virus on this. Give me a minute . . ."

Andy shot a glance at the clock: just a little over one hour until midnight. Invisible fingers began to tighten around his neck and he shook them off. There was still time; he wasn't sunk yet.

"Okay," said Lester, "it looks like there's only one thing on the disk. It's a bitmap."

"A what?"

"A bitmap. An image."

Andy shook his head. "What does that mean?"

Lester took off his glasses and massaged his nose with a dramatic sigh. "A bitmap is like a picture or a graphic. It could be a photograph from a digital camera or an image of something that somebody scanned. I need to check it for viruses before we open it."

"How long will that take?"

Lester swiveled in the chair. "A lot faster if I didn't have to keep stopping to answer questions."

"Sorry."

Lester turned back to the computer and started typing. "I don't know why I bother trying to be the nice guy all the time. All people do is take advantage. The only time Debbie calls is when she wants something."

"That's not true," Debbie said quietly.

"Whatever." Lester pushed away from the desk. "Okay, it's done."

Andy bent forward and stared at the screen. It was a picture of a lake with an arrow pointing into the middle of the water.

"It looks like the arrow was drawn on with a marker," said Lester, tapping the screen. "My guess is that someone took the picture with a camera, drew the arrow, and then scanned the image."

"What does it mean?" Debbie asked.

"This is what you so desperately needed to see?" Lester asked. "If you wanted to see the lake so badly, you could have just driven there. It's only a couple of miles away, and it's the same one that . . . well, you know . . ."

Lester looked at Debbie. She was staring into the floor with her arms crossed.

"What?" Andy croaked, already knowing the answer.

Lester fidgeted in the chair. "You know . . . it's the lake where . . . Craig . . . drowned."

Andy stared at the screen. That was it, then. Craig had been true to his word and led him to the end, just as promised. And somewhere at the bottom of the lake was the final prize, waiting to be collected.

"Will this help Kate?" Debbie asked.

Andy gave them both a final, helpless glance before staggering into the hallway. The sound of crazed laughter filled his head, and he didn't know if it was Craig's or his own.

56

Kate opened her eyes and immediately let out a shout; something hard was pressed against her chest and she couldn't feel her legs. She jerked back, and sharp pain shot into both wrists, sending hot needles up her arms.

All at once, everything came rushing back: she was in the woods, sitting on the ground with her arms and legs wrapped around a small tree. Her wrists were bound together by rope on the other side.

"You took a long sleep."

She turned her head with a startled cry. He was sitting in the bed of Andy's pickup with one leg hanging over the side. Threads of shadow and light flickered across his face from the campfire.

"I was startin to wonder if you was gonna pass out," he said. "Shit, you ain't slept since yesterday. I pulled up about fifteen minutes ago and you didn't even stir."

Kate pursed her lips and said nothing.

"Silent treatment still, huh?" He laughed. "Kinda old for that, ain't ya? Must be somethin you picked up from them school kids, I guess."

She turned away in disgust. He knew things about her. Where she worked, where she lived . . . even the type of car she drove.

"I saw your brother while you was sleepin," he said. "He ain't much of a talker either. It don't bother me none, though. Me, I like the quiet. Sometimes I come out here and sit for hours by myself. Course, other times I come out here and scream my head off when I'm pissed, just like you did about a half hour after I left."

Kate opened her mouth in surprise but caught herself before anything came out.

"Oh, yeah, I heard ya yellin. I was just parked over that hill, takin a moment to myself before drivin back into town." He laughed. "My favorite was 'He's crazy, someone help!' Course, *your* favorite was just plain old 'help.' I counted at least fifteen of those."

He considered.

"Maybe it was twenty. Shit . . . I lost track after a while. I prolly forgot to mention we're bout thirty miles in all directions from anything. So go ahead and scream more if ya like. I don't mind. Speakin of screamin, check this out."

She looked away as he held out his wrist, but not before catching a glimpse of a crude tattoo.

"That there is a snake," he told her. "Inked this one myself right here in this very field. Hurt . . . like . . . a . . . *mother*. I screamed my ass off for that one. But that one didn't hurt nothin like this one."

He showed her the back of his neck. Two Chinese symbols were set just below the hairline. He caught her looking and grinned.

"Like that, do ya? Yeah, all the ladies go nuts for shit like that. It's Japanese for 'danger.' You know, like saying 'Do not touch.'"

He laughed and plucked the cigarette from his mouth. It disappeared into the darkness with a quick finger flick.

"It was a girl," he said proudly. "Some little Japanese whore I used to run with. She thought a tat would look cool there. I always joke that since I don't know Japanese it prolly means 'shithead' or somethin like that. Too bad you teach kindergarten instead of Japanese. Course, you'd prolly lie to me about what it means anyway. Why wouldn't you?

Here I am, keepin you against your will and all that. Well, I reckon we can fix that."

He slid out from the bed of the pickup.

Kate cried, "If you so much as touch me—"

"*Please*," he said with a chuckle. "I already told ya I ain't gonna hurt ya, and I sure as shit ain't interested in anything else. Even if you was my type, you're so old it'd be like pokin my mom or somethin. And I don't know why you're all bent out of shape with me. It ain't like this is my fault."

Kate's mouth dropped. "How is this not *your* fault?"

"Shit, it ain't like I never been inside Craig's house before, lookin around. If you hadn't showed up, I would've just snuck on out like always. So it ain't my fault you was at the wrong place at the wrong time. So now I guess you're like insurance."

He grinned at the thought.

"Yeah . . . just like insurance. And as long as I get what was promised to me, there won't be no problems. It's not like I'm gonna kill ya. I ain't no monster."

He gave her a wink that sent goose bumps down her arms.

"There are some monsters round these parts," he said. "A few years ago this one lady killed her husband for cheatin. Shot his balls clean off with a shotgun. She even made the kids watch as he bled to death right there on the kitchen floor. Then she turned the shotgun on them and shot them dead, too, prolly 'cause they reminded her of him. That there is some harsh truth. And when the cops came, she didn't even try to run or nothin. She just sat there, like she was waitin for someone to come and take her out for dinner or some shit. Cripes, some people are too dumb to know what's good for 'em."

He squatted by the fire and started feeding sticks into the flame. His eyes glistened in the glow.

"Yeah, I got me lots of stories. Course, I don't reckon you're too interested in much of what I got to say. Then again, maybe somethin a little closer to home might perk things up. Maybe somethin that happened right here in town. Yeah . . . that might be interestin. We got nothin better to do than pass time, right?"

He settled onto the grass and brushed off his hands.

"Poker," he told her, "is the best game in the world. Ain't nothin else like it. Chance, skill, and luck, all rolled up in one. Me, I can't get enough of it. Love it. Every Saturday night we play poker in Keota, rain or shine. Ain't no more than a few of us, but sometimes we'll find some fresh blood, just to shake things up.

"So a while back one of the boys brings up this new guy, and let me tell ya, this guy was quite the sight. He talked in a funny voice, drove a moped, and always seemed all keyed up and shit. But he seemed okay enough and he had money, so we cut him in.

"So pretty soon he starts comin every week. We'd always rip him a load of shit for the moped, but he never minded. He was funny that way. He never minded much of anything.

"But this one night . . . I ain't never seen him so down. He didn't say nothin during the game, not one word, and he was drinkin more than the rest of us put together. Pretty soon we ran out of beer, and him and me got elected to go get more. He always had money to buy shit like that, so I was more than fine to tag along and do the carryin.

"So we're walkin to the store, and he still wasn't talkin, but it didn't bother me none. I mean, it wasn't like we was best pals or nothin. We just played cards together, ya know?

"So we get the beer, and he finally starts talkin, and says he won't be comin to the games no more. Says he has a tumor in his head that's gonna kill him in a couple months."

Kate could feel his eyes on her, waiting for a reaction. She forced herself not to look at him.

"I laughed when he told me, thinkin he was just screwin around like he did sometimes. Then he sat down right there on the curb and started cryin, just like a little girl. Started ramblin on about all kinds of crazy shit. Mostly about this old geezer he worked with at the graveyard and his granddaughter. Said they hated him and he didn't know why. Then . . . then he started talkin about his daddy."

Kate lifted her head.

"Well now," he grinned, "I guess I do have somethin interestin to say after all, huh? Oh, yeah . . . he got real keyed up talkin about his daddy. Sayin how the dude wasn't dead and he knew who he was, and he was never gonna forgive his mom for what she done. Then he got this weird look in his eyes, like he was somewhere else in his head, thinkin about stuff. And not good stuff either. I tell ya, at that moment, watching him sitting there, rubbin his hands together so hard his knuckles were turnin white . . . shit, it was almost creepin me out."

He clapped his hands together and Kate jumped.

"Damn, all this talkin is makin me hungry. Got any food in that heap of a truck?"

She let out a small, trembling breath as he stood and went to the cab. She didn't believe any of it. He was toying with her, playing games. It was all lies and she wouldn't—*couldn't*—let herself get sucked in.

"Well, looky here," he said with a laugh. "Ain't we fancy?"

He was twirling a piece of cloth around his finger, and Kate's mouth dropped when she realized it was a pair of underwear from her bag.

"Hey!" she shouted. "Stop—"

"And what else we got here?"

Her mouth closed with a snap when she saw the pregnancy test in his hand.

"Well, that's a funny kinda thing to pack when visitin. Hopin for a little action, was ya?"

A small click escaped her throat. She clenched her teeth to stop anything from coming out and stared furiously into the dirt.

"Tell you what," he said. "I'll finish up my story and we'll come back and talk more about you, deal? Oh, and you ain't got shit to eat neither."

He tossed the pregnancy test in the bed of the pickup and fished out a beer. "You thirsty yet?"

She narrowed her eyes and glared at him.

"Suit yourself." He pulled the tab, took a long drink, and let out a loud belch.

"So we're sittin there, and he keeps talkin and talkin and gettin all worked up. Said he was tired of bein around it all, he was gonna die anyway, so what was the point? Said if he was gonna die, it was gonna be on his terms.

"But here's the kicker. He said he was too chicken to do it himself, so me bein drunk and prolly not really meanin it, I says to him, 'I'll do it.'"

Kate took in a papery breath. His eyes were on hers, challenging her to speak. She couldn't have drawn away her gaze even if she wanted to.

"He didn't say nothin, and after a while I got bored and got up and left him. The boys needed beer and I was tired of babysittin. He never came back to the game, but he called me later that night. Asked if I was serious 'bout what I said. Said he'd make it worth my while. Shit, I didn't know what to say. I mean, it wasn't like I would be doin it to someone who didn't want it, but if I got busted then my ass was back at lockup."

He shook his head and uttered a small laugh.

"But then . . . then I hear this little voice right there in the back of my head. That ever happen to you? Ever hear somethin like that?"

He paused, actually waiting for Kate to answer. She looked away in disgust.

"It says to me, 'Harlan, you're livin in your daddy's trailer and wor-kin at the car wash. What have you got to lose?' So I started thinkin on how nice it would be to just up and leave and never look back. And only a fool would walk away from easy money."

He paused to drink from his beer.

"So there it was," he said, lowering his voice. "All the cards on the table, just like when we played poker. Then he asks me how much. Now I know he ain't rich or nothin, but he always had money for poker, not like some of them other guys. One time he brought damn near two hundred bucks.

"So real casual like, I says, 'Ten thousand.' I know that ain't a fortune, but it also ain't nothin to fart at. Part of me's thinkin he's full of shit, and another part's thinkin there's no way he had that kinda money . . . but I figure that's what it would take. And you know what? He didn't even think or act surprised; he just says okay. Just like that. Then he did that old movie trick where they say in a real serious voice, 'You get half now and half later.' But shit, if we was gonna do this thing, it wasn't like he was gonna be around later to pay me. Know what I'm sayin?

"But he says don't worry about it, it's taken care of. So I figured, what the hell? Even if I just got five thousand it was better than nothin. He told me he had to set up one last thing, and then we'd do it. One last thing, he said, and then it would be time. And the rest, as they say, is history."

He drained the can and crushed it in his hand.

"You're lying," Kate said in a trembling voice. "Craig fell off a cliff."

"Hey, I don't give a shit if you believe me or not. It don't change the facts."

"What *facts*? We don't even know you—"

"And yet you're fallin in love with me," he said. "I can tell."

"What?" she cried. "What . . . why . . ." She was so furious she couldn't even speak.

"Shit," he laughed. "I was just playin with ya. You're so serious. Just go with it. Have some fun."

"*Fun?* You kidnap me, tie me to a tree, and now you tell me you murdered my cousin for money? You think any of this is *fun?*"

He shrugged. "Daddy always said you have to deal with what life gives you. So deal."

"You're sick."

"Hey, I didn't ask for any of this. This here was Craig's idea. I'm just along for the ride, tryin to make a livin. And as long as your brother gives me what's mine, we won't have no problems."

"What?" she cried, suddenly close to tears. "What do you want from us?"

"I don't know why you two keep playin dumb," he said sharply. "All it's doin is pissin me off. Craig told me. He said on Friday the thirteenth his cousin would come to town and bring me the other half of my money."

"Money?"

"Craig was a real joker, all right. When he showed up with half the money, I was thinkin it was gonna be five thousand dollars. But he gave me all ten thousand right then and there, all of them brand new hundred-dollar bills."

"And all of them cut in half, right down the middle."

"I was plenty pissed about it. He said this was the only way it could be done, and if I wanted to call it off then he'd get someone else. He said his cousin was comin to town and bringin me the other half on Friday the thirteenth. Sort of like deliverin it."

Kate's face had gone sheet white. "Andy."

"Shit, at that point I really wanted to kill him for messin with me, so I figured I might as well go ahead. What else was there to do? So I got nothin until your brother gives me the other half."

"And Andy has to . . ." A wave of nausea passed through her. "That's the game. That's what he has to find."

"Find?" His face wrinkled. "What's this *find* business?"

"Andy doesn't have it," she said hoarsely. "Craig left a dead rat under the fridge and we found a key. Then he had to break a lamp . . ." She tried to pull together her thoughts. "Why would Andy keep money that's cut in half and worthless? He doesn't have it."

"I been watchin your brother since he came to town, and he's been doin some weird shit. Seen him sneakin all around, climbing trees . . . One night he was even diggin inside the shed at the new graveyard. Are you tellin me that's him looking for the other half of my money? The money that was promised to me?"

"Yes!"

"'Cause Craig hid it somewhere."

Kate nodded fervently. "Yes."

He took off his cap and stared at the sky. Kate realized she was holding her breath and let it out between her teeth.

"It's the truth," she said.

He grunted. "That's somethin, all right. I sure hope he finds it. For your sake."

"No," she said, shaking her head. "He can't find it."

"Lady, that ain't my business. My business is gettin my money, and that's what I expect to do."

"But he can't—"

"*Hey*, you can jabber all ya want, but that doesn't change nothin. Maybe you're telling the truth and maybe you're lyin, but I don't care. I just want my money so I can go away and forget all this shit. Once I get my money I'll be happy."

"Happy?" she cried. "You're going to be on the run for the rest of your life for a lousy ten thousand dollars!"

"Okay," he said, his voice wavering for the first time, "you need to shut up now. What's done is done. If you keep talkin, I'm gonna lose my temper, and you don't want to see me lose my temper. It ain't pretty."

He tossed his empty can into the fire and went to the pickup. Kate closed her eyes, wanting to throw up. For the last four days, all she had done was tell Andy not to play the stupid game . . . and now Andy's only chance was to finish the game and find what was at the end. And if he didn't, this guy would think he was lying and kill him. The game had never been about money . . . This whole time Andy had been playing for his life.

"Time to get movin." He was standing over her, his face taut and serious. "It's past eleven thirty. You need to pee before we go?"

"I'm fine," she answered stiffly.

"You ain't peed for a day. I've givin ya this one chance. It's now or it's gonna be runnin down your leg at some point."

She glared up at him. "I said I'm *fine*."

He drew a switchblade from his pocket. Kate let out a shriek and frantically started pedaling at the dirt.

"Hey!" he shouted. "Don't be stupid. I'm just gonna cut ya free."

He bent down and held her forearm firm. The stench of alcohol wafted to her nose as she turned away, her whole body shaking.

"Stay still," he warned, "or this is gonna end bad."

Her hands curled into fists as the blade cut at the rope. She shut her eyes, fear escalating into terror as she waited for the pain of steel against bone—

The rope snapped and her hands sprang to her chest. Her shoulders came alive with pain and she let out a small moan.

"Here's what's gonna happen," he told her. "All this shit you're tellin me is hurtin my head, and I got to cover my bases. It's all about insurance, like we talked about. All I want is my money. But I need to know how much leverage I got. You get me?"

Kate swallowed, afraid to speak.

"So you're gonna pee. I ain't askin; I'm tellin. You can go and squat behind a bush, and I promise ya I won't watch. That's my word. But I also promise that if you run off I'm gonna catch ya and you're gonna be sorry. You believe that, don't ya?"

She nodded.

"Then let's get this over with."

He held out the pregnancy kit.

"No," she said, horrified.

"I told ya, I got to know how much leverage I got. Two lives is more important than one. That's all this is about. It's like a business transaction. You're gonna do it; then you're gonna show me."

He shoved the box into her hands. She stared at him with wide eyes, shaking her head.

"Please," she whispered. It was almost a sob. "We don't have to do this."

"We can do this the easy way or the not-so-easy way. The easy way is me stayin over here while you go over there by them bushes."

"We'll lie," she pleaded. A shimmer of hope rose inside her. "When we go see Andy I'll . . . I'll pretend that we did it and go along with whatever you tell me to say."

He grinned at that. "Naw, you won't be in the same frame of mind. I want you like this. Besides, the truth is much more fun than lyin, don't ya think? And ain't you just a little curious now? I sure am."

"Please . . ."

"Two lives is more important than one. If I got this on my side, then I know he'll make the right choice. So go on. Don't make me ask again."

"I can't—"

"I'm givin you this one chance to do this alone," he said in a stony voice. "If need be, I'll be the one standin there holdin it. You better *believe* I will."

The box trembled in her hands as her eyes filled with tears.

"Go on, now." He batted a hand at her. "Shoo."

Somehow she got to her feet. Her legs quivered in protest as she struggled to maintain her balance, and when he grabbed her by the elbow she let out a loud sob.

"No farther than them bushes," he told her. "Be quick."

He gave her a shove and she stumbled forward with a cry. The tears came hard and fast as she put one foot in front of the other, not daring to look back. Every inch of her body had gone cold.

She stopped at the edge of the bushes, furiously wiping her eyes with one hand and clutching the box in the other. There was no way she could do this . . . She couldn't . . .

She closed her eyes and imagined herself back home. Back at her apartment. She was standing in front of the bathroom sink, staring at her reflection in the mirror. Her period was late. In her hand was a pregnancy test. She was going to take the test, and it was no big deal. She had done this before. It was no big deal . . . She could do this. She could . . .

Her fingers blindly began to pick at the corner of the box, trying to work open the seam. Tears streamed silently down her cheeks.

She never heard him come up behind her.

FRIDAY THE 13TH

57

Andy stared numbly at the clock as the second hand inched past midnight. He was out of time and out of options. The kid was coming back for something Andy didn't have, and there was nothing that could be done to stop it. The kid was not going to be reasoned with. He was not going to be swayed by talk. And when the kid didn't get what he wanted . . .

The doorbell rang and Andy sat paralyzed as the sound hung in the air, suspended for an eternity. He rose on wooden legs and started down the staircase. It didn't register as to why the kid would be ringing the bell until he opened the door and saw Debbie on the front step.

"What are you doing?" he cried. He shot a frantic glance down the street. "You can't be here."

"You ran off without saying anything. What about Kate?"

"She's fine, but you need to go. Right now."

"I don't understand."

"Debbie, it's—" *Not safe* was how he meant to finish. The words locked in his throat as two headlights popped into sight from the end of the street. They were moving fast and with purpose.

"Is that her?" Debbie asked.

Andy shook his head without taking his eyes from the truck. "No. We need to get inside."

"Why? Who is that?"

The truck was closer now; in another few seconds they were going to be in its headlights.

"Debbie, you have to trust me."

"But—"

"Please!" he shouted, making her flinch. "Debbie, *please.*"

"Okay," she said sullenly, moving inside. "But I don't understand what the big deal is. Who is that?"

He barely had the door closed before the truck pulled into the driveway. "Go upstairs and out the back door. Do it now and don't look back."

"But I don't understand."

He grabbed her by the arm and pulled her up the staircase.

"Ow," she whined, "you're hurting me—"

He slid open the patio door. "If you care anything about Kate, go right now."

"But—"

"Go!" he shouted, pushing her through the door and slamming it shut. He plunged down the stairs, two at a time, and reached the front door as it swung open.

"Here I am," Harlan said cheekily. "As promised."

"Where's Kate?"

"That depends. Where's my money?"

And just like that, there it was: *money.* The prize was nothing more than cash.

"What's it gonna be?" Harlan asked. "I'm a busy man. Got places to go and people to visit."

"How much?"

"Shit . . . you really gonna stand there and tell me you didn't even look at it? I ain't no idiot. Now you best give it, or my ass is back in your truck and you won't like your sister too much when you find her. I promise ya that."

"I can get money."

"I don't want *your* money; I want *my* money. The money that was promised to me. The other half of them bills."

"Listen," Andy said, holding up an unsteady finger. "It doesn't have to be like this. Craig . . . he screwed us both. He took the money and hid it—"

"Spare me the sob story. Your sister was tryin to sell me this same shit."

"I swear," Andy said, heat rising in his belly. There was no way it was going to end like this, not after everything he had been through. "Craig set up these clues . . . I had to figure them out . . . He tried to get me to dig up his body, for God's sake."

Harlan regarded him with a cool stare. "Are you tellin me my money is buried there with Craig? Buried there inside his coffin?"

Andy started to shake his head . . . Then all at once everything clicked. If he could buy more time, he could figure this out. Talk his way out of it.

"Yeah," Andy said huskily. "Buried in his coffin."

"Somebody would have seen it. Somebody there at the funeral place."

Andy dry swallowed, carefully fitting the pieces together before he spoke. "It was hidden away. Inside a book. His favorite book. The pages of the book were cut out . . . The money was inside. It's there for the taking. I couldn't do it . . . couldn't bring myself to dig it up. It's not the sort of thing a person just does."

"Bullshit. You just stick the shovel in the dirt and toss it away. That ain't hard."

"Then help me," Andy said. "We'll do it together. You get your money, I get Kate, and everyone wins."

Harlan studied him. "You're messin with me."

"What have you got to lose? Do you really want to walk away

empty-handed? It's so close, right there, waiting for us to take it. Craig is the enemy, not you and I. We can outsmart him by helping each other. Don't you see that?"

Harlan was silent.

"It doesn't have to be like this," Andy said. He was almost pleading now. "Everything that's happened since Craig died . . . It was all his idea of a morbid joke. He wanted to punish me, and you got dragged into it. He's been playing us against each other since the beginning. I don't want the money. I just want my sister."

The kid continued to stare. He wasn't buying it, and even if he did, then what? Did Andy really think stalling was going to give him time to think of a master plan and somehow turn the tables? He was kidding himself.

"Okay, then," said Harlan.

Andy forced himself not to swallow. "Okay?"

"We best get movin. Takes time to move dirt. You got a shovel?"

"Yeah," Andy said after a pause. "It's outside."

Harlan held open the door. "Lead the way."

Andy hesitated, all at once certain the kid was going to whack him over the head the moment his back was turned. He almost welcomed the thought; at least it would put an end to this nightmare.

They passed through the doorway. The night air had turned cool, but he barely felt it; everything was moving quickly now, and he needed to stay alert. Stay focused.

"Don't mind if I drive, do ya?" Harlan asked with a grin.

"Sure," Andy muttered absently. The shovel was leaning against the garage where he had left it, and he almost dropped it twice trying to get it into the bed of the truck. His palms were rivers of sweat.

"Let's go!" Harlan was already in the cab, keying the engine to life. "Rock and roll!"

Andy climbed inside and barely had the door shut before the kid stomped on the gas, knocking both of them back in their seats.

"I do like this truck," Harlan said with a grin. "Thinkin about takin it with me when I leave town. I'm guessin you're okay with that."

Andy closed his eyes and frantically tried to get hold of his thoughts. He had his time . . . Now he had to figure out what to do with it. The cemetery was no more than a mile, and he could feel the panic boiling up inside him—

"This is crazy," he blurted out. "Let me give you the money and we can forget all this digging business. Does it really matter where the money comes from?"

"You got the money now?"

"In the morning. I can go to the bank."

Harlan laughed. "You expect me to believe you're gonna walk into the bank and leave with ten thousand dollars?"

"Craig had tons of insurance," Andy lied. "I inherited everything he owned. I can get money. I just need one day."

"Or we wait another hour and dig it up. Me, I vote for the diggin. Hold up . . . You best grab on to somethin . . ."

Harlan gunned the engine as they approached the intersection.

"Hey," Andy said, clawing for the seatbelt. "Wait—"

Harlan cranked the wheel, and the truck slid violently around the corner, all four tires screaming for purchase.

"Hot damn!" Harlan shouted.

The truck straightened out and Andy put his hands to his face.

"You are one sad sight," Harlan said with a grunt. "Ain't no wonder you couldn't dig up that coffin: You got no balls for nothin."

They passed through the cemetery gates. The headstones outside flew past in a blur of headlights.

"Fifteen thousand," Andy said in a strained voice. "As soon as the bank opens."

"*Fifteen!*" Harlan cackled. "This just keeps gettin better and better! I also kinda like Craig's house. How bout throwin that in to sweeten the deal?"

"Anything," Andy said. His voice had become a painful croak. "Just talk to me and let's figure this out."

"Anything, huh?"

"Yes!"

Harlan slammed both feet into the brake pedal and the truck slid to a stop. For an absurd moment Andy thought the kid was actually going to listen to reason . . . Then he realized they had reached Craig's grave.

"What I want," said Harlan, "is for you to get your ass out of the truck and get your damn shovel."

Andy swallowed. "If we could just—"

"I ain't gonna ask again." His face grew dark as he bore into Andy with his eyes. "We can do this the easy way or the not-so-easy way. I don't reckon you'd like the not-so-easy way."

Harlan grabbed the flashlight from the dashboard and climbed out. The engine was still running, and Andy stared incredulously at the keys dangling from the ignition. His heart began to thud inside his chest as his mind chased this information: all he had to do was slide over, drop the truck in gear, stomp on the gas—

"Vamoose!" Harlan shouted, pounding on the hood.

Andy gave the keys a final glance as he opened the door. He wasn't going to drive off any more than he was going to try to catch the kid off guard and overpower him. He was a coward and they both knew it. He was going to do exactly what the kid wanted him to do, and after that . . .

After that he didn't want to know.

The kid was on the far side of Craig's grave, looking out into the darkness. Andy reached blindly into the bed of the truck for the shovel and instead felt something soft, almost like clothing—

"Jesus," he hissed, jerking back. The thing was moving, and he realized in horror it was a person lying flat.

"It's me," said a hushed voice. "Debbie."

"Debbie?"

"I'm here to help," she whispered. "I snuck in here when you were talking inside the house."

"Hey!" Harlan bellowed. "We ain't got all night! Get your ass in gear before I come back there and drag you over here!"

"I'm . . . I'm coming," Andy stammered, trying to keep his voice steady.

He pleaded with Debbie with his eyes as he lifted out the shovel, and it took every ounce of his will to pull himself away.

"You and your cousin like games, huh?" Harlan asked. "I got a game for ya. I'm gonna go get smokes and road beers, and you got until I get back to get this dirt moved. And if I don't see my money when I get back, I'm gonna beat you to death with your shovel. Then I'm gonna drive me to Luther and find me some other family to beat. That sound like a good game?"

"Why do we have to do this?" Andy cried. The words trembled on his lips as despair and anger rose inside him. "It doesn't have to be like this! It's just *money*. I . . . Twenty thousand. I can get that. All in cash—"

"You know somethin? You're just as pathetic as Craig: beggin even at the very end. He never stopped beggin, even when I was holdin his head under the water."

Andy's blood ran cold. "Craig fell off a cliff."

"Yeah, pushin him off was supposed to do the job, but it didn't. He was all messed up and bloody and shit, but he wasn't dead. So I just held him underwater till he stopped movin. But I never hit him or nothin. I just held him down. Cops would see marks on his body and shit. I ain't no idiot."

Harlan spit in the dirt.

"So don't treat me like no idiot. You ain't got no money at the bank, and I'm pretty damn sure there ain't no money buried in this ground. For your sake, you best prove me wrong. But do it like a man."

Harlan started for the truck. Andy stared at the ground in a half trance, too stunned to speak. Not suicide . . . The kid had pushed him . . .

The truck door slammed.

"Debbie," he whispered.

His eyes searched wildly as the kid sped off, looking for any sign of her, praying she had crawled out and was hiding nearby.

"Debbie!" he screamed.

The only response was the wailing of the wind.

The shovel dipped in his hands as Andy heard it again: the faint but unmistakable sound of an approaching vehicle. A moment later two headlights came into sight, and all the strength ran from his legs as the shovel fell from his fingers. It was over. He had barely moved any dirt, and even if he had managed to get to the coffin, it wouldn't have changed anything. They both knew there was no money there, no treasure beneath their feet. He could try and stall an hour or a day or a month, but it made no difference.

The headlights splashed over the hill, blinding him with light, and he took a step back as the truck slid to a stop across from him. He barely had time to register the truck wasn't his before Ricky Simms climbed out, holding a shotgun.

"Hey," Andy said. "Hey, wait—"

"You bastard," Ricky said. His voice cracked as he moved forward. "I warned you. As God as my witness, I warned you not to mess with my family."

"I didn't—"

"Lester Hatcher's daddy called me. Said some guy was over at his place with Debbie. I know it was you. And I knew if I looked around this godforsaken town long enough I'd find you trying to hide somewhere. You tell me where she is. You tell me . . ."

Ricky's eyes fell on the broken dirt. Horror dawned across his face. "You buried her?" Ricky choked.

"*What?* No!"

"You buried her," Ricky said again. This time it wasn't a question. His chin began to tremble. "You had your way with her and then buried her with that bastard cousin of yours—"

"Listen to me," Andy said, holding out his hands. "This isn't what it looks like."

"Then where is she?" Ricky demanded. He raised the shotgun and leveled it at Andy's chest. "You tell me!"

A horn blasted. They both turned toward the headlights bouncing down the path at them. The vehicle skidded to a stop next to Ricky's truck, and Andy felt a sickening drop in his belly. There was no mistaking whose truck he was seeing this time, or who was inside. Things had just gone from bad to worse.

"Old Man Simms!" Harlan shouted out the window. "You best be movin on! Me and him got some unfinished business here!"

Ricky raised a hand to block the light. "Harlan Shawler, I should have known scum like you would be hanging out with the likes of this one! I seen you around town, knowing you were up to no good!"

"I'm serious, now," Harlan shot back. "You don't want to mess with me. I got me some insurance. I found me a little spy in the back of the truck."

"*Grandpa!*"

Ricky's throat made a clicking sound. "Debbie?"

Harlan got out of the truck, pulling Debbie behind him. He marched her into the light with one hand around her elbow and the other around the nape of her neck.

"You let her go!" Ricky shouted. "You let her go right now!"

"I don't think so! Not with you wavin that shotgun all over the place. You're mighty keyed up and I don't reckon I can trust you. You best toss that thunder stick over to me."

"Don't!" Andy shouted.

Ricky brought the shotgun back on Andy. "Harlan, you let her go now! Do it or he's a dead man!"

Harlan pealed out laughter. "Shit, I think we got us a standoff here. I got somethin you want, he's got somethin I want, and you got the only gun."

"I'll pull this trigger!" Ricky warned. "So help me!"

"I think you're bluffin, but go ahead and shoot his face off if ya want. Me and him is the best of buddies, but you do what you gotta do. You pull that trigger. You do that and I'll let you have Debbie back. I don't need her anyway. Whaddaya say?"

"I don't know him," Andy sputtered. "He's lying—"

"I'll do it!" Ricky screamed. "I'll kill him right here and now if you don't let her go!"

"Are ya deaf, old man? I'm *tellin* ya to do it! Do it and I'll let her go!"

"Grandpa!" Debbie wailed. "Don't—"

"You got three seconds!" Ricky told Harlan.

"You're wastin my time," was Harlan's reply.

Andy closed his eyes as the barrel of the shotgun sank into his chest.

"One!" Ricky hollered.

"He killed Craig," Andy moaned.

"Two!"

"*Grandpa!*"

"Three—"

"Old Man Simms, *you're wastin my time*—"

The hammer on the shotgun clicked and Andy screamed.

"Son of a whore," Ricky muttered. "Son of a . . ."

Andy fell to his knees as his leg muscles broke into convulsions. He stared down at himself in awe. There was no hole, no blood.

"Are you shittin me?" Harlan roared with delight. "The damn thing wasn't even loaded?"

Andy lifted his head; everything around him slowed to a crawl.

Ricky was bent over the shotgun, fumbling with the shells inside. Harlan was laughing hysterically. Debbie's shoulders were jerking side to side, as if Harlan was shaking her . . . and then Andy realized she was working herself free of his grip. The next thing he knew she was bringing her knee up into Harlan's groin.

The world caught back up to speed.

"Goddamn!" Harlan screeched. His lips pulled back in a grimace as he cupped both hands over his crotch. "Oldest damn trick in the book."

Andy scrambled to his feet as Debbie ran toward them. She grabbed Ricky by the arm, and he shook her off and advanced on Harlan.

"Wait," Andy croaked.

"Quite a fire demon ya got there, Simms," Harlan said with a pained grin. "I can see why Craig was so fond of her."

"Which one of you touched her first?" Ricky shouted. His breath came in sharp bursts as he swung the shotgun back and forth between Andy and Harlan. "Which one?"

Andy held out his hands. "I'm begging you . . . You don't know what's happening. This piece of shit has my sister. If you shoot him, then she dies."

"Yeah," said Harlan, "so you can't *touch* me."

"Which one? Tell me!"

Harlan said, "You ain't got the balls to use that thing—"

"Shut up!" Andy screamed at him. "Shut your mouth!"

"She's just a little girl," Ricky said in a strangled voice. The shotgun wavered in his hands. "How could you?"

"She's a woman now," Harlan said with a grin. "Had me some fun with her on the ride over—"

The shotgun exploded. Harlan's body flew backward through the air and hit the ground in a writhing pile.

"Oh shit," Andy whispered.

Debbie began to scream. Andy barely registered this; he was unable to draw his eyes away from Harlan. The kid's hands flapped at the air, as if conducting a disjointed symphony of the stars above. His chest and face were peppered with blood.

"Kate," Andy whispered.

Kate was somewhere else, and the only person who possessed that information was splayed out on the ground in front of him.

Harlan was no longer moving.

"You killed him," Andy said numbly.

He spun around just as Ricky snapped the shotgun back together.

"Bastard," said Ricky Simms.

The shotgun exploded again.

SUNDAY

58

Kate let out a startled cry; Harlan was in front of her with both hands locked around her neck, his face twisted in anger as he began to squeeze—

"No," Kate gasped, bolting upright.

Her hands frantically went to her neck, trying to pry away his fingers . . . but there was only her gown, crumpled to one side and doused in fresh sweat. She was still in the hospital, safe in her room.

"Another bad dream, hon?"

Kate turned with a start and saw Cindy in the doorway.

"No," Kate said. "Well . . . not too bad."

"Not too bad, my *butt*." Cindy came into the room and set her clipboard on the bed. "Amanda said you had at least two on her shift last night."

Kate shrugged and summoned a smile. "I see you brought your twin sister with you to work again today."

"Don't get too attached to her. I know you don't believe me, but your double vision will go away eventually."

"In a few days or *weeks*," Kate said with a groan. "You'd think in this day and age you'd have a pill to cure that."

"In the meantime, why don't you tell me your name?"

Kate sighed. "We both know that I know my name."

Cindy shook the bottle of water in her hand. "If you don't answer my questions, you don't get this delicious, refreshing water."

"If you want to tantalize my thirst, you'd at least offer me wine or something along the lines of a soda."

Cindy lowered her eyebrows.

"Fine. Kate Anne Crowl."

"Date of birth?"

"And why is this necessary again? The doctor said I have a concussion, not amnesia."

"Think of it as extra credit from an overly concerned nurse. Birth date?"

"Fifth of August."

"Siblings?"

Kate frowned. "Like either of us could forget that one."

"Good enough." She surrendered the water. "Now outside of hating your nurse and seeing two of everything, how else do you feel?"

"I'm tired of having a headache."

"Well, honey, getting whacked over the head with a big rock will do that to you. Don't make me tell you again how lucky you are you have a thick skull."

"Twenty stitches lucky."

"Yeah, and another twenty minutes of lying unconscious in that field and you might not be here right now. Count your blessings, girl. Wounds heal. It's just a good thing that shithead didn't hit you any harder than he did."

"Language," Kate said, unable to hide a grin.

"Yeah, well . . ." Cindy plucked up the clipboard and held it to her chest. "Clifford Albright called a bit ago to check on you."

"He did? That was nice of him."

"I can get him on the phone if you'd like. He left his number."

Kate considered. "Thanks, but I still think I'd like to wait and visit him in person. I figure that's the least I can do for someone who found me bleeding in the middle of nowhere and saved my life."

"It's too bad the only reason he was out in the woods in the first place was to kill small, innocent animals."

"Now, Cindy," said Kate, "we've been over this before. Squirrel hunting is in season right now, so what he was doing was perfectly legal."

"That still don't make it right. Men and their guns. It's a good thing he didn't accidentally shoot *you*."

"Amen," Kate agreed. "Speaking of that, and I'm almost afraid to ask . . . how is Andy today?"

"Oh, he's been hollering for you again. I swear we've never had a patient—one who *isn't* in a constant amount of pain, mind you—make as much noise as he does. Does that boy ever just sit still and stay quiet?"

"Not too much."

"You ready to start taking his calls again?"

She knew what he wanted; he'd been a broken record about it for the last two days.

"Or we could change the subject completely," Kate said brightly. "How's life outside these prison walls? Any exciting plans tonight?"

"Oh, absolutely. After this I get to wait for my son to pick me up. Provided he doesn't forget again. Kids are the gift that keep on giving, you know. The gift of headaches, money problems, gray hair . . ."

Kate dropped a hand to her stomach. "Please, don't hold back how you *really* feel."

"Oh, your little one will be a darling. They're bundles of joy the first couple years anyway."

"He—or she—has already been a joy. I've been more nauseous in the last few weeks than I have in the last few years. It's a special bond we have."

"Have you told the father yet?"

Kate's gaze wandered and fell.

"I'm sorry. I didn't mean to pry."

"It's . . . complicated."

The phone on the table rang and they looked at each other.

"Do you want me to tell him you're sleeping?" Cindy asked. "I don't mind."

"Oh now, we mustn't lie. But if you were to sneak into his room and accidentally yank the phone cord from the wall after this . . ."

"Done and done."

Kate picked up the phone. "Hello, Andy."

"They're still letting you out today, right?"

"Yes."

"Promise me you'll call as soon as you watch it. How are you getting to the house? Is Mary driving you?"

"Yes."

"Remember, it should still be sitting by the video player. It's a black videotape with no label. I can't believe I was so stupid. The floppy disk was just a ruse; I'm sure of it. The videotape is the real clue. Whatever is on tape is the key."

"Andy," Kate said quietly. "Does it even matter? It's over."

"Of course it matters. What if there's more—"

"Andy, you're lucky to be alive! The first shell misfiring in the shotgun, the buckshot from the second shell only clipping your hip and thigh . . . You might walk with a limp for the rest of your life; have they told you that?"

"Of course they have."

"And still, all you care about is this stupid game. Let it go. Haven't we been through enough?"

She stopped herself then. She wasn't going to let him do this to her again. Not now. Not ever.

"You still don't get it," he said.

"Get what?"

"It's not *finished*," he said, dropping his voice to a whisper. "The money is still out there—"

Kate slammed down the phone so hard it bounced off the table and fell onto the floor. Cindy picked it up with a chuckle.

"You were nicer that time," she said. "Didn't cuss once or anything."

"Please tell me I'm getting out of here in the next hour so he can't keep calling me."

"Won't be much longer," Cindy assured her. "I need to finish making my rounds. I think I saw Mary in the cafeteria a bit ago . . . Want me to send her in now?"

"That's okay. I'll find her when it's time to leave."

"You know, I knew your aunt before I moved here to Keota."

"You're from Mortom?"

"Born and bred. Stayed there until I was eighteen, then came up here for school. Mary used to substitute teach at the high school sometimes."

"Really?" This was news to Kate. "What did she teach?"

Cindy produced an almost queer smile. "Gym. Mary was a tough old bird: never let anyone slack and made sure everyone gave a hundred percent. Most of the kids despised her, but I respected her for being so hard on us. I always figured she was just getting us ready for life. There was always a core confidence about her, like she was a woman who knew what she wanted and stayed the course. Determined. It's easy to see how the two of you are related."

Kate looked away, slightly embarrassed.

"My folks left Mortom years ago," Cindy said. "I don't get back there too often—no reason to—but sometimes on the weekends I'll drive through, just to see if anything has changed. And it always looks the same. Not much really happens there. Well, not normally."

Kate cleared her throat. "Has there been any word on Debbie or her grandpa?"

"Not according to Mary. Not since they were seen driving out of town. But Mary said the police are positive they'll catch up to them before too long. She also said he would never hurt his own granddaughter, so don't you fret about that."

Kate forced a smile.

Cindy squeezed her hand. "Sure you don't want me to get Mary?"

"I think I'd just like to be alone for a little while."

"You get some rest," Cindy said with a smile. "I'll shut the door on my way out so you can have some quiet. And we'll hold all your calls, *especially* the ones that originate from inside the hospital."

"Thank you. Thank you for everything."

"You just worry about taking care of that little miracle," Cindy said, lingering at the door. "And don't forget to send us a picture when the little darling is hatched."

"I will."

She rolled over to her side, her hands going to her stomach. A new beginning.

A new life.

Nothing had ever sounded so good.

"Are you sure you want to do this?" Mary asked again.

They were parked in Craig's driveway, staring at the house.

"Let me go in for you," Mary said. She gave Kate's arm a squeeze. "Just tell me what you need from inside, and I'll go and get it."

"Thanks, but I promised Andy that I'd do this. It's . . . important. To him, anyway."

"I don't want to know, do I?"

"Probably not." Kate opened her door and steadied herself before climbing out. "I shouldn't be too long."

Mary said, "At least let me help you inside."

"It's okay. Really." She pushed out a smile. "I'm fine."

Mary gave her a weary nod. "I'll be right here."

Kate shut the door. Her smile crumbled when she turned to the house. She was miles from fine. The last time she had been here was the night Harlan had taken her. If she never set foot inside again, it would be too soon, but Andy was right about one thing: This needed to be finished. Not for the sake of the game or money, but because they needed to move on with their lives. And if this was what Andy needed for closure, she could do that. But this was it. After this she was done, and it was up to Andy to decide what to tell their parents when they arrived back home.

She started up the steps with her gaze firmly on her feet. If she looked across the street, she knew she would lose it. The Simms house was nothing more than a news story now: "Local Man Shoots Two People before Kidnapping Granddaughter and Fleeing Area." The whole town was talking, but no one knew much. The only thing anyone was absolutely sure of was that Harlan Shawler was dead. No one seemed to care too much about it.

She pulled open the door. It probably was stupid of her to go this alone (if for no other reason than her double vision), but it had to be done. And the sooner it was done, the sooner it could be forgotten.

She used the railing to help her up the staircase. The videotape was sitting on the player, just as Andy said it would be. All the answers were there . . . or so he believed. But maybe some things were better left untold. Nothing good had come with anything associated with the game, and she didn't expect this to be any different.

The phone rang and startled her into a shout. She scowled at the kitchen, knowing it was Andy. Now he would keep calling until she answered. Regardless, he was going to have to wait.

She fed the videotape into the player and powered on the television. The screen went blue, and she took a step back, hoping beyond hope the tape was blank and there would be nothing—

"Greetings and salutations," said a squeaky voice.

The hairs on the back of Kate's neck stood on end as a figure stepped into frame. Even with blurred vision there was no mistaking it was Craig.

"So here we are," he said mildly. "If you're not a complete fool, then you're viewing this tape directly after locating it in the locker. But if I were to lay out cold hard cash, I'd be willing to wager you took the videotape back to my house and found the computer diskette. I imagine you were plenty irate upon viewing it, thinking I had cheated you. But what's a little humor between *cousins*, right? It was all in good rivalry."

He leaned forward and clasped his hands together.

"But that's all the past. Now you need to concern yourself with the future. If you're viewing this, it means you did some truly abhorrent things, like unearthing my grave. And if you did that, then you absolutely deserve what I am about to bestow on you. If you haven't deduced yet, it's money. But it's not for you; it's for my associate, Harlan. He'll be coming for it on Friday. Hopefully you're viewing this before then, because he's not going to be pleased if you haven't acquired it. He has a bit of a mean streak."

There was a sound and Kate turned her head. Mary was at the staircase, and Kate quickly moved forward to turn off the television.

"Don't," Mary said.

"I have a brain tumor," said Craig. "Do you know what I did when I first found out? I phoned you. For some inane reason I actually thought you might care. I left a message on your machine that it was urgent to call me. I'm sure you remember, because the next day I phoned again. Same message. I left a message every day for a week, and you never returned one call."

He raised both hands with an exaggerated shrug.

"But no matter. I still had Mary and Ricky Simms to share my pain. Ricky Simms resides across the street, as I'm sure you've learned. I was like a son to the man, and he became like a father to me. It was a beneficial arrangement, because as we all know, my real father died in a car crash before I was born. Or so I was told my whole life. In fact, that was the only thing I was ever told about the man. You see, no matter how much I implored or pleaded, Mary would never tell me anything else.

"Shortly after I found out about my tumor, I swore an oath to myself. I swore that before I left this foul earth I would know *something* about my father. Some physical feature, some mannerism, some activity he enjoyed . . . something to help me understand who I was. Truly, how could she deny me this one tiny request?"

Mary let out a sob. Kate flinched without taking her eyes from the screen.

"She refused me," Craig said flatly. "She said it was for my well-being. She said nothing positive would come of it, and it would only cause me pain and suffering. That's what she said, and she stood firm.

"But I wouldn't give up.

"I was relentless, refusing to let it go, determined to wear her down. Day in and day out I asked. Guilting her at every opportunity, throwing my impending death in her face every chance I got. Every conversation we had, no matter what the subject, I would find a way to turn it back to my father. A few details, that's all I wanted. Was that too much to ask? Was the truth really so horrifying? All I wanted was to know where I came from. To know who I really was. So finally, I told her I suspected the truth. I had always suspected it.

"Ricky Simms was my father."

Mary was in tears now, her whole body trembling.

"Ricky Simms," Craig said again. A small, cryptic laugh escaped his mouth. "What a fool I was."

Mary said, "Turn it off—"

"And sadly," he said, "that was finally what it took to unlock the truth. All my begging and threatening . . . None of it mattered to her. But the moment I told her I believed Ricky was my father . . .

"Let's just say Mary is a prideful woman, and her pride runs so thick, so *deep*, that the very thought of me believing that Ricky Simms was my father . . . It was too much for her to bear."

"Please," said Mary.

"And with that, she finally disclosed what I so longed to learn. Are you ready for it? You're going to love this. So much so that I'll give you a hint, just to give it a little time to sink in."

"No," Mary sobbed.

Craig said, "We're brothers."

"What?" Kate cried.

"Brothers," Craig said again. "You and I share the same father, is what I mean to say. Apparently the man had an affinity for nailing sisters in the same family."

"It wasn't like that," Mary moaned.

"But I got the shit end of the deal," Craig squealed with a crazed laugh. "You got to live in the city with a mother and father, while I was just a dirty little secret, swept under the Mortom rug. *My* mother wasn't good enough for your father—"

"I tried to explain," Mary said. "He wouldn't listen—"

"And I hated him," Craig said, baring his teeth. "As soon as she told me, I hated him for it. And I hated her for lying about it my whole life.

"But most of all, I hated you.

"I hated you for having the life I never had, and all the opportunities I was never given. You weren't some weird kid who lived with his weird mother, stuck in a weird little town. And if that wasn't injustice enough, all I ever heard from my mother was how I should be more like my *perfect* cousin. And the pathetic part is that I tried.

"I tried because I wanted to be liked by you and loved by her. I wanted to make her happy. Make her proud. But I was a fool. It soon became obvious she loved you more than she loved me, her own son."

Mary whispered, "I never meant—"

"I hated you because you brought out the worst in me. You always brought out the worst in me. I tried to live my life fair and just, while you simply breezed through everything, never giving a shit about anything but yourself. And it wasn't fair that I was going to die and you were going to live. It wasn't fair that you got to live the life I should have had. It wasn't fair that everyone thought you were better. We were brothers, not cousins, and you weren't better than me."

Craig lowered his head, breathing heavily.

"And then I knew what had to be done. If I proved I was smarter than you, then everyone would know who the better man was. So I set up the game for you to play, with very simple rules . . . and very high stakes.

"If you followed it to completion, you would live. And if you didn't, then you would join me in death. Of course, I couldn't be entirely sure what Harlan would or wouldn't do, but he didn't know about the game. And I knew if you tried to explain it, he wouldn't listen. He is . . . shall we say, a simple man.

"But that's neither here nor there. The fact remains that I gave you a fighting chance for your life, which was more than this shitty world gave me. Your game was fair. If you failed, it was your own fault, not mine."

He straightened up.

"Down to business. The money is in the driveway, hidden inside the trunk of the station wagon. Look for a thick, cardboard envelope shoved under the spare tire. Ten thousand dollars, cut down the middle. It should be easy enough to match up the serial numbers and tape them back together. I hope for your sake you didn't have the car towed.

"That's it. Show's over."

Craig walked out of the frame. A moment later the picture went black. Kate stared at the screen, trying to find some words. *Any* words.

Nothing was forthcoming.

"My God," said Mary. "I don't . . . I didn't . . ."

She sat on the couch and folded her hands in her lap. Her face was stark white and her eyes were glassy balls in their sockets.

"I don't know what to say," Mary said quietly. "I don't even know where I would begin."

"Is it true?" Kate asked. Her voice sounded far away and faint to her ears. "What he said about his . . . about our . . . father?"

All at once it hit her: If Craig and Andy were brothers, that meant Craig was *her* brother as well.

Mary met her eyes. "It's true."

"*How?*" she cried in a voice that was barely more than a whisper. "How could he . . . How could you . . ."

She lowered herself to the fireplace hearth as she gaped at Mary, utterly speechless.

"You know some of the story," Mary began softly. "You know I moved to Luther to start college before your mother. You probably *don't* know that I met your dad before your mother knew he existed. He lived in the dorms across the river from me, and each day we'd pass each other on the way to class and chat a spell. Pretty soon we started keeping time on the evenings and weekends. Everyone thought we were a couple, and even though we never spoke about it aloud, we both knew we were together. Nothing serious, mind you, but we were serious enough to . . . Let's just say we were young and dumb and not too worried about babies and things like that."

Kate felt her cheeks flush.

"Then your mom came up to start school. I introduced them, and he pretty much took to her right away. Your mom, bless her heart, tried her best to keep her feelings hidden, but it was pretty obvious she felt the same way as he did. Me, I wasn't so much looking for romance and marriage and all that excitement, so I quietly stepped aside. It was pretty clear they were meant to be together, so I didn't fret over it too much. I was happy for both of them, and I just put it behind me. Until I came up pregnant, that is to say."

"Mary," Kate whispered.

"But I didn't hold it against him," Mary said sternly. "No, sir. I was as much responsible as he was. It was just bad timing and bad luck. Course, if I hadn't met him, he might never have met your mother, and then you kids wouldn't be here today. So I guess saying it was bad luck ain't quite fair. But however you looked at it, what was done was done, and somehow things needed to be put right for everybody. And with that, we decided the best thing to do was not tell anyone."

Kate swallowed what little saliva she had. "Mom doesn't know?"

"Oh, your mother knows," Mary said. "It was your *dad* we decided not to tell. Your mom was my sister. Family is family through thick and thin. I told your mother about it the second I found out. There was never any doubt in my mind I needed her to know. But your dad . . . He was so full of kindness and compassion . . . It would have just made things complicated.

"Your mother and I made the decision together not to tell him. Right or wrong, that was our choice. That took care of the first problem. The next problem was more of a challenge. It didn't take long for people to notice I was putting on weight, and once I did . . . let's just say your dad looked awful nervous. He never flat out asked me anything, but he said plenty to your mom about it. So finally I told him. I told him it wasn't his. I told him it was from someone else . . . and your mother stuck by my side and told him the same."

Mary offered a wan smile.

"After that the only smart choice was to quit school and focus on raising the baby. School was never really for me anyways, and I never really cared too much for Luther. Problem was, I was too proud to move back to Keota. Back in those days it was looked down upon to be pregnant with no husband. So I settled here in Mortom instead. I could be close to my family and raise Craig in a small town. The first time someone asked about Craig's daddy, I told them he was killed in a car accident. Didn't even really think on it; it just sorta came out. And from there on, that was my story. And I knew one day Craig might ask to go see the grave, and that was why the poor man died in Canada. Way too far to travel up there just for something like that. Craig . . . he never was one for traveling very far. He was more content to just stay put."

Mary nodded, her eyes sparkling.

"But your mom and dad . . . they were great. They came up every weekend to help out the first few months after Craig was born. I always wondered if maybe your dad suspected, or maybe your mom told him and made him promise not to let on, but whatever the case, your dad never once complained about giving up his weekends and never once acted out of sorts around me. I like to think he still doesn't know, and that's just the type of man he is. A good man full of love."

She trailed off, her face grave and full of sorrow.

"So many times," Mary said, her voice choked with tears. "So many times I wanted to tell Craig everything I just told you. And I never had my chance. After I told him who his daddy was, he wouldn't let me say anything more. Wouldn't let me explain. He barely let me talk to him at all. And he died thinking his daddy was a bastard who didn't want him, and I couldn't do anything about it. I gave up trying to tell him . . . I didn't want to be fighting our last few weeks together. And now he's gone forever, and he'll never know."

The phone rang and they both looked up.

"It's Andy," Kate said.

"What are you going to say?" Mary asked in a thin voice.

Kate sat without moving. Didn't their father have the right to know he had lost a son and not a nephew? Would Andy want to know he had lost a brother, not a cousin? Would it matter? Would it change anything?

Kate slowly rose to her feet. Mary's lips moved soundlessly as she went into the kitchen and picked up the receiver.

"I'm here."

"Did you find it?" Andy stammered.

Kate's eyes went to Mary, who was hunched forward with both hands pinned under her chin.

"The tape isn't here," Kate said.

"What? It *has* to be."

"Just let it go, Andy. It's over."

"Harlan . . . he must have come back and taken it after he left the cemetery. He must have known what was going on the whole time. Dammit, how I could be so stupid—"

She hung up the phone and looked at Mary.

"I'll wait outside," Mary said softly.